BANISHED FROM THE HERO'S PARTY,

I Decided to Live a Quiet Life in the Countryside

6

ZAPPON

Illustration by **Yasumo**

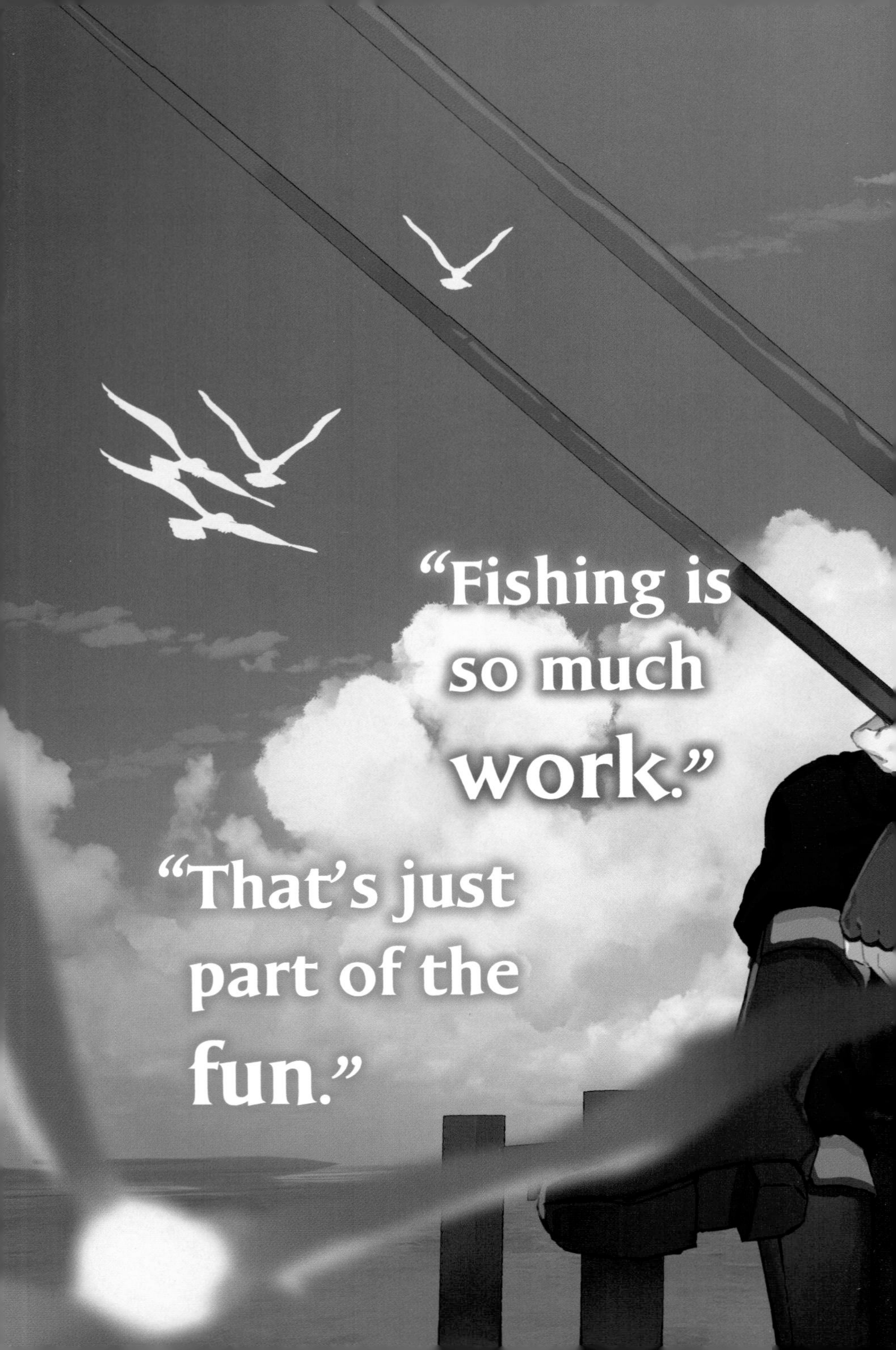

"Fishing is so much work."

"That's just part of the fun."

CONTENTS

"That's my line, Red... Please leave this to me."

“I’ve been
wondering
who was
lurking in
the dark
so
stealthily.”

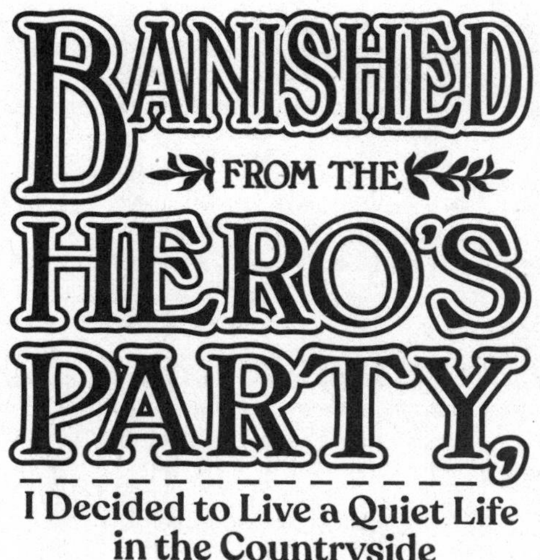

I Decided to Live a Quiet Life in the Countryside

6

ZAPPON

Illustration by
Yasumo

New York

Banished from the Hero's Party, I Decided to Live a Quiet Life in the Countryside, Vol. 6
Zappon

Translation by Dale DeLucia
Cover art by Yasumo

▼▼▼▼▼▼▼▼▼▼▼▼▼▼▼▼▼▼▼▼▼▼▼

Yen On
150 West 30th Street, 19th Floor
New York, NY 10001

Visit us at yenpress.com
facebook.com/yenpress
twitter.com/yenpress
yenpress.tumblr.com
instagram.com/yenpress

First Yen On Edition: June 2022
Edited by Yen On Editorial: Jordan Blanco
Designed by Yen Press Design: Andy Swist

Yen On is an imprint of Yen Press, LLC.
The Yen On name and logo are trademarks of Yen Press, LLC.

▼▼▼▼▼▼▼▼▼▼▼▼▼▼▼▼▼▼▼▼▼▼▼

Library of Congress Cataloging-in-Publication Data
Names: Zappon, author. | Yasumo, illustrator. | DeLucia, Dale, translator.
Title: Banished from the hero's party, I decided to live a quiet life in the countryside / Zappon ; illustration by Yasumo ; translation by Dale DeLucia ; cover art by Yasumo.
Other titles: Shin no nakama ja nai to yuusha no party wo oidasareta node, henkyou de slow life suru koto ni shimashita. English
Description: First Yen On edition. | New York : Yen On, 2020.
Identifiers: LCCN 2020026847 | ISBN 9781975312459 (v. 1 ; trade paperback) | ISBN 9781975312473 (v. 2 ; trade paperback) | ISBN 9781975312497 (v. 3 ; trade paperback) | ISBN 9781975312510 (v. 4 ; trade paperback) | ISBN 9781975333423 (v. 5 ; trade paperback) | ISBN 9781975343248 (v. 6 ; trade paperback)
Subjects: CYAC: Ability—Fiction. | Fantasy.
Classification: LCC PZ7.1.Z37 Ban 2020 | DDC [Fic]—dc23
LC record available at https://lccn.loc.gov/2020026847

ISBNs: 978-1-9753-4324-8 (paperback)
978-1-9753-4325-5 (ebook)

1 3 5 7 9 10 8 6 4 2

LSC-C

Printed in the United States of America

CHARACTERS

Red (Gideon Ragnason)

Kicked out of the Hero's party, he headed to the frontier to live a slow life. One of humanity's greatest swordsmen with many feats to his name.

Rit (Rizlet of Loggervia)

The princess of the Duchy of Loggervia. A truly happy young woman who grew out of her more combative phase. She uses spirit magic, and can summon wolves and transform into one.

Ruti Ragnason

Red's younger sister and possessor of the Divine Blessing of the Hero, humanity's strongest blessing. Free at last from her blessing's impulses, she now enjoys life in Zoltan as a medicinal herb farmer while adventuring on the side.

Tisse Garland

A young girl with the Divine Blessing of the Assassin. An elite from the Assassins Guild, she is taking a break from her usual job and working together with Ruti to get their medicinal herb farm running.

Yarandrala

A high elf Singer of the Trees capable of controlling plants. Unlike Red and the others, she is still a hero who actively seeks to resolve the troubles she encounters.

Mistorm

An old lady with the Divine Blessing of the Archmage. A former hero who protected Zoltan. Yarandrala saved her when she was attacked by a group of covert killers.

Salius of Veronia

The eldest prince of the Kingdom of Veronia. His place in the line of succession dropped when his mother, Queen Misphia, disappeared from the palace.

Lilinrala

A high elf with the Divine Blessing of the Pirate. Fleet Admiral of Veronia and former captain of the Elven Corsairs. She has come to Zoltan in search of someone.

Prologue

A Villain's Divine Blessing

All living beings in the world, except the Asura demons, were granted a Divine Blessing at birth by almighty Demis. Divine Blessings bestowed strength in the form of levels and skills, allowing frail creatures like humans the ability to fight giants and monsters on equal terms. Were it not for Divine Blessings, people would have perished long ago.

That was what the village priest said to the kids gathered in the little holy church. Children were struggling to sit still and listen, and every once in a while, one would poke the person next to them and start messing around. Among the restless kids, Ruti and Gideon sat quiet and proper.

Rather than thinking them well-mannered, the priest felt unnerved by their maturity.

A charming young boy named Tapp raised his hand. "Mr. Priest! Why do monsters have Divine Blessings? Aren't they bad?"

Monsters came in many forms, and to say that all were evil was an over-generalization. Still, it was true that the majority of them were harmful, and many savage monsters attacked people for sport, not survival. What's more, there were beings with blessings that could truly be called wicked—demons. Undoubtedly, everyone had thought at one point or another that humans and elves would be better off if evil beings didn't possess Divine Blessings.

The priest, whose Divine Blessing was Adept, had asked the same question in this very holy church when he'd been a child.

"The answer to that lies in our own Divine Blessings, Tapp."

"In ours?"

"Divine Blessings grow when a bearer kills another with a blessing. But if there were only good and righteous people in the world, then whom could we slay? God wishes for us to live more righteously by fighting evil. That is why God gave the wicked Divine Blessings."

Tapp nodded at the priest's answer, seemingly understanding. The young boy who had connected with his Fighter blessing proudly declared, "I'm gonna kill even more monsters!"

His blessing was level 3. He already regularly went out with adults to hunt monsters with his spear and bow.

"Excuse me…," a voice called as a small hand rose in the air. It was soft, yet it still carried a strength to make itself heard, despite the rambunctious kids. Other children quieted down and cautiously looked at the girl that had spoken.

"What is it, Ruti?" The priest recoiled slightly. It was the first time that mysterious girl had ever posed an inquiry.

"What is the reason for impulses?"

"Hm, ah, yes. That's a good question."

The priest patted his chest as he breathed a sigh of relief. The purpose of impulses was self-evident, tautological. It was akin to teaching that one and one made two. It comforted the priest to know that Ruti was fairly normal on the inside, even though she was odd.

"As you all know, Divine Blessings have urges. My Adept blessing motivates me to protect everyone's peace of mind and to use my magic to aid the suffering. It was those impulses that led to my becoming a priest."

His blessing also discouraged new thinking and prioritized conservative ideals, but the priest decided there was no need to mention that part.

"The Divine Blessings that God has granted us bestow tremendous strength. Our impulses keep us from using that power recklessly and guide us along the path we should walk in life. Obeying your blessing's urges grants a sense of security in your heart. That is the key to living a happy, righteous life."

Hearing that, Tapp clenched his fists with determination. He would later go on to beat down all the boys in the village who liked to fight, becoming their tyrannical leader. It all started with what the priest had said.

Undoubtedly, the priest's words had a strong influence on all the children.

Ruti's expression remained placid, however.

* * *

Time passed, and Gideon and Ruti were now fighting on their own.

Villagers were being evacuated in the face of an attack by the demon lord's army. At present, Ruti was resting at the feudal lord's manor.

An inauspicious feeling struck the girl, and she picked up the magic blade that her brother had given her. A single large bat was hanging from the ceiling. Ruti immediately pointed her sword at the creature. In response, the bat grinned and dropped to the floor.

There it transformed into a human and bat hybrid, with bat-like wing membranes extending from its arms. This was an animal transformation skill, but that was not what surprised Ruti.

"You're...human?"

Her opponent was neither an orc nor a demon. It was a human with an Assassin blessing.

Ruti had never fought against another human before during her journey to stop the demon lord's army.

The hired killer wielded a sinister, twisted shortsword. It was a brutal weapon that magnified the pain of those cut by it, though to Ruti, it just looked challenging to wield.

A grin formed on the half-bat's face.

"Pretty girl, those red eyes of yours will make an excellent addition to my collection."

Ruti didn't reply, instead listening coolly to the assassin's little speech.

His present state was undoubtedly a result of the impulses of his Assassin blessing blending with his own desire to imbue his work with a sense of artistry. This man took pleasure in killing people. Thus, he was an enemy who had to fall.

Ruti readied her sword, determined to fight.

The battle ended with her killing the one who had come to take her life.

That day, the Hero's level rose by 1, for a total of 10.

Chapter 1

The Veronian Galley

A day had passed since the solstice festival.

I headed to the plaza in front of the city gates to go fishing like I'd promised Tanta and the others.

"It's fishing time!" Tanta said.

"Yeah!" I raised my rod in reply.

Rit, Ruti, Tisse, Tanta, and I had all gathered.

"Hm? Where's Gonz?" I asked.

"Uncle Gonz drank too much at the festival yesterday. He said he'll pass for today. I think he's sleeping off the hangover."

"It was his idea to go fishing in the first place."

"He took your medicine, so I think he'll be all right by lunchtime."

Sheesh.

"Fine then, guess we'll just go ourselves."

Tanta nodded excitedly. "Okay!"

Perhaps he'd been worried that the trip would be canceled because of Gonz? He laughed as I patted his head to reassure him.

"I've got food for everyone, too," Rit said as she held out the large basket she was carrying. Numerous foods had been packed into it. I had made them all, of course. "So, where are we going?"

"I was thinking we could maybe rent some horses and ride to the sea," I replied.

"In that case, Rit and I can summon some spirit beasts," Ruti stated.

"Is that okay with you, Rit?" I asked.

"Of course!"

With that settled, we ventured beyond Zoltan's gate. We'd set out from town on a journey to the Wall at the End of the World a few days ago, but it was for a far more relaxed trip this time.

Once we were out of the town, Rit summoned a pair of spirit dire wolves, and Ruti conjured two spirit steeds. Rit's wolves rivaled bears in size, and Ruti's horses had beautiful white coats and came equipped with saddles and reins.

Tanta looked shocked initially, but he quickly settled down. One of the wolves carefully grabbed Tanta's clothes with its mouth and lifted him onto its back.

"So cool!" Tanta was petting the spirit beast's fur excitedly. Evidently, he was enjoying himself.

"I guess you're good there then. I'll ride with you." I hopped up onto the wolf's back, sitting behind Tanta.

"Are you sure? Wouldn't the horse be better since it has a saddle?" Rit questioned.

"We'll be fine," I assured her.

The dire wolf snorted in response to Rit's worrying, as if to say, "Leave it to me."

Tanta grew even more excited at that. His eyes were sparkling as he clung to the wolf's neck.

* * *

Simply put, fishing was profound.

Of all the skills in the world, there were only three related to it—the common skills Fishing and Angling, and the inherent skill Advanced Fishing. That last one was only available to blessings like Fisher and Angler.

I'd taken the Fishing skill and raised it to level 3. Doing so granted me Improved Visibility Through Water. The effect was pretty self-explanatory. It let me ignore light diffraction and allowed me to peer through the cloudiness of the water for a clearer view. It was likely intended for spotting how many fish were beneath the surface.

The common skill Swimming granted some maneuverability and a bit of battle aptitude in the water, but it did nothing for your eyesight. Aquatic Combat also provided access to Improved Visibility Through Water and was the superior skill overall. While it was available to the vast majority of fighting-oriented blessings, it was still an inherent skill, which meant I couldn't get it.

Battling while submerged was difficult. Armor became a hindrance that kept you from moving properly, and swinging weapons was all but impossible. Thrusts were the only halfway usable attacks with swords. The best choice was to avoid underwater combat if you could help it. Some situations left you with no other alternative, though. There were countless monsters dwelling beneath the surface, just like there were up on land, and both fishing and shipping over the water were necessary aspects of our lives.

One of the reasons it was difficult to navigate around the Wall at the End of the World by sea was because storms frequently plagued the waters to the east of Zoltan. A more significant reason, however, was because that region was infested with giant sea monsters.

Krakens, deep sea serpents, great whites, and luscas all prowled the region. Even worse, there were Sea demons, familiars of the legendary Leviathan demon, which were capable of changing shape into giant aquatic dragons.

If a ship were attacked from below, there'd be no recourse but to dive into the water and dispatch the creatures on their terms, which was all to explain why I had the Angling skill and was pretty good at fishing.

"All right, got another one."

I was dropping the fish I caught into a container filled with seawater, one after the other. I had landed six so far.

"Ghhh."

Rit was glaring at her bobber floating on the surface.

Skill or no skill, if you allowed your intentions to leak out that much, no fish was going to approach.

We were on a jetty not far from Zoltan. It was a small port used to offload goods from merchants who traveled around coastal villages. There were fees to use Zoltan's docks, so the traders who went around peddling day-to-day necessities loaded and offloaded their boats here.

"Ruti."

"What?"

"Throwing your hook into the water and hitting a fish with it isn't Angling."

Ruti already had more than thirty fish in her container. She wasn't baiting her line at all. Instead, she cast the hook so that it landed in her target's mouth and pulled it out.

It was an absurd brute force method, but effective nonetheless. Ruti was reeling in fish from the seabed, fifty meters down. She hadn't missed yet, so I couldn't fault her method, but it could hardly be called fishing.

"But it's faster this way."

"I mean, yeah, but..."

Ruti looked at me incredulously. She'd never done this before, so I wasn't too surprised.

"Okay, I'll teach you how to fish," I decided, standing up. "When you take a day off to go fishing, the goal isn't to catch anything; it's to have fun."

"How so?"

I adjusted Ruti's rod, then picked a blue worm for bait. The little things were easy to come by, and fish liked them. Some people didn't like the way blue worms wriggled, though. I threaded a bobber and sinker onto her line and then hooked the blue worm.

"This is the basic method for baiting your line. Generally speaking, it's best to make sure it's snug on the base of the hook," I explained.

Ruti nodded earnestly. "Okay."

"You don't have to throw it too far away. Just toss it close by and then wait patiently for the fish to come."

"Really?"

"If you throw it with too much strength, the worm might come free, and the fish we're dealing with here aren't that big. Threadfish can pick bait clean off the hook, so you've got to check your line occasionally. For now, just toss it right in front of you and take it easy."

"Fishing is so much work."

"That's just part of the fun."

Ruti took the rod back and cast again. The bobber floated gently atop the waves. A bird cawed overhead.

"The weather's nice."

"Mhm."

The colder months made the ocean frigid, but beautiful.

When winter came to Zoltan, the winds from the Wall blew out to sea, and the surface water would shift from the coasts toward the open ocean. Conversely, deeper water rose to the surface.

Even without my skill, the water appeared a clear blue. It was easy to spot the red fish swimming around. Knowing the reason behind this phenomenon did nothing to mar its allure.

"Such an amazing thing to see," I muttered as I looked out at the ocean.

Rit and Ruti, both struggling for different reasons, gazed upon the lovely vista with me.

"Zoltan is great."

"It sure is."

They both had tranquil smiles on their faces.

* * *

"How about we take a break for lunch?" I suggested.

Tanta was the first to respond. "Yay! I was starting to get hungry."

"Gah, it's not like I was going to catch up to you anyway," Rit pouted playfully.

Turning to my sister, I asked, "What about you, Ruti?"

She stared at the bobber floating on the water before reluctantly reeling it back in and setting her rod down.

"It was fun."

Ruti had only reeled in two fish the proper way. Honestly, that was exceptional for a beginner. Still, I had been slightly worried that the more laid-back nature of proper Angling would bore her. It was a relief to see she'd enjoyed herself.

Initially, she'd seemed perplexed at not getting many bites, but she settled into the pleasure of kicking back and waiting.

On that point, Tisse was something else. She'd only caught a single fish, but it was so big that it couldn't fit in her container.

Tisse had paid no attention to the small fires and had set her sights on the big score. At first glance, it may have seemed she was only casually casting her line, but she was truly proficient.

We gathered around the picnic basket.

"What did you make?"

"All sorts of things."

Inside the basket were sandwiches, a tomato salad, omelets, roast beef, ground steaks, and milk to drink.

"Ohhh, it's all so colorful." Tanta immediately went for some roast beef.

Rit took a ground steak, while Ruti and Tisse started with some of the salad.

"""""So good!"""""

My effort in the kitchen this morning had all been worth it to see their smiles.

When we had nearly finished everything, Tanta suddenly pointed out toward the water.

"Look over there! It's a ship!" he exclaimed.

Following the direction of his finger, I spied a galley with two square sails being rowed systematically by oars that looked like countless legs extending from its sides.

"That's a warship."

And not a Zoltan one. Zoltan's armed forces only possessed three caravels with triangular sails, so there was no mistaking it.

"...A vessel from Veronia or thereabouts, I'd guess?"

Observing it closely, I noticed that the uppermost of the three layers of oars had noticeably fewer rowers than the lower tiers. Such a design was unique among galleys from southern nations like Veronia.

Its deck was set higher than most other ships' so that when it lined up alongside an enemy boat, they could fire a volley of arrows from on high. Veronia had designed this model around eighty years ago for dealing with pirates who primarily relied on melee combat. However, Veronia had converted their old-style galleys into large sailing ships in more recent times.

"They aren't pirates, right?" Tanta asked nervously.

"It's certainly possible, but raiders around these parts wouldn't have such massive boats." Plus, Danan had supposedly sunk no small number of pirate ships on his journey here. The buccaneers would be lying low for a while. "There's no way a galley will survive the eastern passage's storms. I wonder what they want in Zoltan."

I chewed on a sandwich as I watched the Veronian warship sailing in the distance, and I pondered what it might be up to.

*　　*　　*

"We should probably start heading back soon," Rit said.

I glanced up toward the sun starting its path down in the sky. "Yeah… I guess it's about time to go."

"Awww. But we can keep going!" Tanta whined.

"If we don't head out now, it'll be dark before we get back."

"Fine… We should do this again, though."

"Yeah, we should all do this together again," Rit agreed.

"Are you okay with that, Ruti?"

"Yes. It was fun. I want to try it another time."

In the end, Ruti caught fewer fish than Tanta once she started actually fishing. Yet it was clear from her reluctance as she packed up her gear that she had enjoyed today.

I was glad that I'd agreed to do this.

* * *

On the morning of the next day, Ruti awoke when she always did. No matter how late she stayed up or how early she went to bed, it was always the same.

"I was able to sleep again."

Ruti's eyes sparkled as the morning sun shone through the window. The simple human action of resting at night was moving to her. Red and Tisse were probably the only ones capable of noticing how excited she was, though.

She rinsed her mouth out with water from the pitcher and then drank from a glass. Then she stripped down and wiped down her body with a damp washcloth. After changing clothes, she started into some light exercise—a loop around the room while doing a handstand. Next, she gripped one of the ceiling beams with her toes. Finally, she hurled a ball out the window, striking a tree in the yard with enough force that the ball bounced back to her. She did this one hundred times with each hand and foot. This was Ruti's daily routine to make sure she was still fit.

"Mhm."

All told, the exercises generally took fifteen minutes.

Ruti did everything at a tremendous speed. Because the Hero blessing always kept her in peak physical condition, the idea that her reflexes might dull, and even the act of warming up, were fresh experiences.

Ruti did not break a sweat through all of it. Her cheeks were ever so slightly red, but that was only because the next thing she had planned for the day was breakfast at Red's place.

Fortunately, no one else knew about the absurd things she considered warm-ups.

* * *

Basking in the morning sun, Ruti and Tisse were walking along the Zoltan streets, headed toward Red's shop.

Tisse had a shortsword concealed beneath her clothes, a carryover habit from working as an assassin. Ruti was not carrying anything. She always left her blade at Red's shop. When she would go out for an adventure, she would make a point of stopping by his store first to get her sword.

Obviously, it was just a clumsy excuse to see Red, but no one seemed to mind.

The neighborhood was a bit rowdy today. People were gathering around the well or in the back alleys, looking concerned as they discussed the latest rumors.

Probably about that warship from yesterday.

The galley would never be able to navigate the stormy eastern passage. That meant it was bound for Zoltan.

What could the crew of such a vessel want in the middle of nowhere?

* * *

"It was delicious."

"Indeed."

After finishing their breakfast at Red's shop, Ruti and Tisse headed to their medicinal herb plantation in the North.

Their meal had incorporated their catches from yesterday: cabbage and fish stewed in tomatoes, an onion and fish marinade, refreshing lemon water, and fluffy white bread.

Both Ruti and Tisse were amazed that Red could throw together so much food so early in the morning.

And also…

"This is the fish you caught yesterday."

When Ruti thought back on how Red had said that to her and eaten the tomato soup with such gusto, she couldn't help but grin.

The manor she and Tisse were living in was on the southwest side of downtown. They'd chosen it to give Ruti easy access to Red and Rit's apothecary, which was nearby. Conveniently, Oparara's *oden* cart was situated at the edge of the harbor district to the west, making it an easy walk when Tisse wanted *chikuwa*.

Ruti's farm was a fair hike to the north, but neither she nor Tisse seemed to mind.

Upon arriving at the plot, the pair had a look around. Ruti's medicinal herb plantation had normal fields and two greenhouses. The latter had glass ceilings and walls on their southern sides to increase the temperature within them.

"There are sprouts, Ms. Ruti."

"Oh. You're right."

Little green seedlings were peeking out from the soil. The nigh-expressionless pair glanced at each other. They were both incredibly moved, but an outsider would never have realized that. Ruti and Tisse shared a deep enough friendship to recognize each other's feelings, however.

"That's fantastic."

"Mhm."

The girls smiled ever so slightly.

*　　　*　　　*

Come noon, Ruti and Tisse were carefully giving the plants just a bit of water, as Red had taught them. They were nearly done with the work. Ruti and Tisse would surely be busy dealing with weeds and pests when the plants began sprouting bushy green leaves. Fortunately, Red had told them that their crops had been cultivated from wild plants, so they should be fairly resistant to such nuisances. In fact, the girls would probably need to keep a close watch on the lines between fields to make sure nothing encroached on other areas.

"That's all for today, right?"

"Yes."

The pair discussed what they'd do for lunch while stowing their tools.

"Pardon me!" a loud voice called out.

Glancing in the direction of the noise, the girls saw Megria from the Adventurers Guild. She must have hurried over, because she was sweating. Had another request from the guild come in?

"Ms. Ruhr! There's something we'd like to ask you to do!"

Ruhr was the alias that Ruti was using in Zoltan. It was a rather shoddy moniker since the full name she used was Ruti Ruhr. Still, it allowed people she was close with to call her Ruti while she went by Ruhr to all others.

It was absolutely critical to Ruti that her older brother, Gideon, address her by her real name. That was something she refused to budge on. Not even God himself could change her mind.

Fortunately, the name Ruti was uncommon enough in Avalonia that anyone would realize the Hero was in Zoltan.

Tisse's alias was Tifa Johnson, and she used Tisse as a nickname.

Ruti wiped her dirty face with a towel and hurried to Megria, who was looking pale.

"What is it?"

"Prince Salius of Veronia has come to Zoltan with a warship."

"Mhm."

Megria was shocked when Ruti nodded calmly at the revelation.

"That's Ms. Ruhr for you. So then you already knew?"

"I saw the galley yesterday, though I didn't know Prince Salius was on it..." Ruti thought back on that name for a moment. "If I recall, Prince Salius is...the eldest son of the Veronian king, but he is the son of the current king and the previous king's elder daughter and was dropped to lowest in succession when the first queen disappeared, right?"

"Yes, that is what I've heard. I'm not particularly well informed on the details, though..."

Megria was just an employee at the Adventurers Guild and couldn't respond confidently. Veronia was a major power, but it was still a far-off nation. The ins and outs of the country's political situation were useless in Zoltan—until yesterday.

"So then, what does the Prince want?"

"He insists we share the holy church registers of Zoltan and the neighboring settlements."

"The holy church registers..."

Holy church registers were written records of the births, deaths, marriages, and notes of residents moving in or out. The documents also listed each entry's Divine Blessing. Clergy used this information to collect taxes for kings and lords while receiving a percentage of the take.

It was required to update the registers for significant life events. Even residents who disliked their taxes put up with it without complaint because the holy church was involved.

A given lord might also keep their own register separate from the holy church's to track the territory and wealth they controlled. The holy church register was only for keeping tabs on people, so it could be used for a per head tax, but not for a wealth-based one.

From time to time, arguments arose among clergy about changing how the records were kept. However, the main goal of the registers was ultimately to assist holy church members, not to collect taxes, so there were currently no plans to change how the records were kept.

"The registers detail our residents' Divine Blessings. The Zoltan clergy were quite indignant at Prince Salius's demand," Megria explained.

Even if they assisted with taxation, the holy church didn't turn over the registers themselves to kings and lords. Salius's request was an outrageous affront.

"I'm surprised he would be so brash. After all, the holy church has a presence in Veronia," Tisse remarked.

The holy church was a tricky organization to deal with, even for the Assassins Guild. Its intelligence network spanned the continent, and it had been a significant obstacle to many a hired killer before.

Megria replied, "Perhaps he thinks word of his action won't reach back home. Veronia and Zoltan are far from each other, after all."

There was something about that that did not make sense to Tisse. The holy church was united in its faith, regardless of national borders. Would the organization truly forgive the prince's insult simply because it happened out on the frontier?

Tisse felt it was unlikely.

"Why does the Veronian prince want Zoltan's holy church records?" Ruti inquired.

"Supposedly...he's searching for someone."

"Who?"

"He refuses to say."

Ruti's eyebrows twitched a little.

"I see. So then it's something unrelated to Zoltan?"

"Yes."

"Then what if we refuse?"

"...Nothing. However, he intends to remain on the water outside Zoltan until he finds the person he's seeking. We were also informed that we need not worry ourselves about their supplies because they'll handle that themselves."

The prince was effectively threatening Zoltan with piracy if the holy church records were not turned over. It was an act outrageous enough to justify a declaration of war. However...

"It goes without saying, but Zoltan's navy is no match for that vessel."

Zoltan's navy consisted of three small caravels, each capable of carrying twenty people. They couldn't stand against the Veronian war galley carrying three hundred soldiers when it came to combat ability. And even if Zoltan did manage to win, there was a distressing difference in power between a major power like the Kingdom of Veronia and a tiny little backwater city-state like Zoltan.

Ruti couldn't imagine that Veronia was plotting to attack Zoltan, but if it did come to war, Zoltan had already lost.

Even if they pled for help with another of the major powers like Avalonia, they had their hands full dealing with the demon lord's armies. They would not have the capacity to spare on a war with Veronia.

In other words, Zoltan was in a situation where they had no choice but to accept the prince's demands.

"Eeep?!" Megria shrieked as Ruti looked at her.

Ruti frantically tamped down her emotions. "Oh, um. I-I'm sorry."

Megria felt the gaze of some giant monster on her for a split second, but after blinking her eyes, she saw that the only other people around were the members of the ever-reliable B-rank party, Ruti Ruhr and Tifa Johnson. She placed a hand on her chest to calm her racing pulse and took a deep breath.

"..."

Ruti was surprised at how much Megria's story had bothered her. She wanted to force her way onto the Veronia ship right that instant, split it in two, and send it to the bottom of the sea.

"What did you wish to ask of me?"

For the moment, Ruti did her best to remain calm and figure out what the Adventurers Guild wanted.

"We'd like for you to participate in the ongoing discussions among Zoltan's leadership."

"Me?"

"Currently, you are Zoltan's strongest fighter. Were a battle with the army out of the question, then Zoltan would have no choice but to rely on your individual strength. That's why we want you to participate in discussions on how to proceed, and we'd be grateful for whatever thoughts you might have, too."

"Okay," Ruti responded immediately.

Megria looked surprised, but answered, "Th-thank you very much. Many adventurers hate these sorts of councils, so I didn't expect you to accept immediately."

"It's okay. Don't worry about it."

During Ruti's time as the Hero, she had frequently been a part of military councils. This was nothing new for her.

Seeing Ruti so at ease filled Megria with respect and awe.

"Where is the meeting being held?"

"At the Zoltan Assembly."

"I see. What is the status of the council?"

"Bishop Shien of the holy church is opposed to acquiescing. Galatine from the Adventurers Guild agrees. Moen, the head of the guards, is on their side as well, and is resolved to fight if necessary. On the other side, Mayor Tornado and Lord William, the head of Zoltan's army, believe a battle is foolish."

"Shien, Galatine, and Moen. They're the old B-rank party," Ruti said.

"Indeed. Perhaps they feel the way they do because they're heroes themselves."

"Thank you. I'd like to listen to what everyone has to say. Let's go."

Megria followed after Ruti as she strolled off gallantly. At some point in their exchange, her fear and dread at dealing with a threat like Veronia had faded away.

What a mysterious person.

Zoltan's newest B-rank adventurer was quiet, rarely showed any emotion, and it was impossible to tell what she was thinking. Her strength was undeniable, though. Even in the direst of circumstances, she and her partner Tisse resolved everything immediately.

At first glance, Ruti appeared less reliable than Rit, Albert, or Bui, but her might far surpassed them all.

Curiously, that didn't feel unnatural or frightening to Megria. When she looked at Ruti, she instinctually believed that the girl would be able to help.

"I hope Ms. Ruhr will stay in Zoltan..."

Megria blushed as she realized that she had accidentally spoken her thought aloud.

* * *

The Zoltan Assembly stood at the center of town.

Mayor Tornado. Baron William, Zoltan's general. Moen, the captain of the guard. Harold, who was the leader of the Adventurers Guild, and Galatine. Bishop Shien from the holy church. These well-known local figures had assembled in a single room with a few leaders from various other guilds.

"Pardon me," Megria said as she led Ruti and Tisse into the chamber.

A few present raised questioning eyebrows. That was more because Ruti was still wearing the clothes she had been while working out in the fields, however.

Baron William made no effort to mask his scorn, but Ruti remained unbothered as she sat in the seat Megria guided her to.

"My name is Ruti Ruhr, and this is Tifa Johnson. Thank you for having us. What is the current situation?"

"Thank you for joining us, Ms. Ruhr." Baron William's vexation only deepened at Ruti's introduction. It was Mayor Tornado who replied to the girl with a smile. "Right now, we are debating how Zoltan should react to the Kingdom of Veronia's demand."

"Have you reached a decision?"

"Unfortunately, it's a rather difficult topic. Typically it would be unheard of for a government to intrude into the holy church's domain, but Veronia seems very determined to find whoever they're searching for. Agreeing to their request would be the best course for maintaining amicable relations between our two nations..."

"Mayor!" Galatine interrupted, staring Tornado down with a twisted, terrifying glare that was better suited to a high-ranking member of the Thieves Guild. "To demand without explanation that we hand over the holy church registers is nothing less than a diplomatic slap in the face. It's an insult!"

Several of the other participants in the council recoiled at Galatine's intensity, but Tornado remained calm. Harold, on the other hand, was breaking into a nervous sweat.

"Galatine, tell me, can honor protect our country?" the mayor asked.

Baron William nodded in agreement. "As the leader of Zoltan's army, let me be clear, if it comes to war with Veronia, we have no hope of winning. Dealing with that single warship out on the water is only barely within the realm of possibility. Were there a second waiting on the sea, I'd suggest we surrender immediately."

"Be that as it may, a demand to turn over our registers is unheard of. That is something the holy church cannot accept. We should request that Father Clemens at the Last Wall fortress make our complaints known to Veronia proper." Bishop Shien's tone made apparent his belief that this was not something he would budge on.

Tornado furrowed his brow and heaved a sigh. Bishop Shien was known for his mild-mannered appearance, gentle personality, and tolerant and forgiving nature. It seemed to trouble the mayor that Shien was having such a difficult time agreeing to turn over the registers.

The Last Wall fortress, huh?

That made Ruti a little bit nostalgic. She had met her comrade Theodora there. At the time, the Hero's party had nearly been declared heretics conspiring with the enemy, thanks to the machinations of the demon lord's army. It had almost come down to a battle with the monks of Demis.

Fortunately, Theodora had believed in the Hero and her allies, ignored Father Clemens's orders, and gone with them. Her aid led them to uncover the conspiracy and resolve the incident.

Oh yeah, wasn't there some secret shrine deep inside the Last Wall fortress that no one had ever entered? We had nothing to do there, though, so I never saw it…

"As stated before, as far as the holy church is concerned, be it the Kingdom of Veronia or anyone else, we have no intention of turning over our records."

While Ruti was reminiscing, Shien had explained that the holy church stood separate from the authority of the secular world and reiterated that his position on this matter would not change.

"I see…" Ruti nodded.

She had a fair grip on the predicament now. Tornado and the majority of Zoltan's leadership believed that they should turn over the records, while Shien, Galatine, and the holy church were adamant about not giving in. Moen had not voiced any opinion, likely because his superior officer, Baron William, was present. From the look on his face, he seemed to be in support of Shien's side.

"I understand the situation. I'd like to comment."

"Ah, Ms. Ruhr. As one of the current B-rank adventurers, I would love to hear your thoughts. You are an adventurer, but please don't let the guild's presence hold you back. I assure you that whatever you say won't hurt your standing," Tornado replied.

"The Adventurers Guild would never do such a thing..." Harold, the head of the Adventurers Guild, wiped the sweat from his wrinkled brow and waved his hands, as if to dismiss the very notion. Then, seemingly experiencing a bout of stomach pain, he took some medicine from his pocket and drank it with a cup of water.

Ah, that's Big Brother's remedy.

The Adventurers Guild was on the north side of Zoltan. Harold wouldn't have gone all the way to the opposite end of town just to buy medicine. One of the local doctors who bought wholesale from Red had likely prescribed it. Harold appeared a rather unreliable sort, but Ruti felt a little goodwill toward him now that she knew the man used one of Red's curatives.

"First of all, we don't have enough information," Ruti stated.

"Information?" Mayor Tornado repeated.

"Their goal, I mean. Who are they searching for, and why? They must have a reason for keeping that a secret."

"We asked, of course. But they've no intent on telling us," Baron William responded.

Tisse grimaced at that. If a party's refusal to answer were always sufficient, there'd be no need for diplomats. For the people of Zoltan, lack of an answer was sufficient, though.

At most, all the Zoltan army dealt with were small bands of thieves or monsters. Actual war was entirely outside Baron William's experience.

"I'll investigate," stated Ruti.

"You will? How?"

"Prince Salius believes that he will learn what he wants from access to the holy church's records. The registers track names, birthdays, current location, job, parents' names, Divine Blessing, and the date of immigration. Among those, names and dates of birth can be faked. If that were enough to determine what they wanted, they wouldn't need to ask for the holy church's accounts. Current location, job, and parents' names aren't necessary when searching for someone. That must mean the one they're after can be identified by date of immigration or Divine Blessing."

"I—I see."

"However, if they know enough to identify this person simply by their date of immigration, they would not need the holy church registers. The prince could simply insist the government hand over their records. That would be far simpler than making an enemy of the holy church. Which would imply that Veronia only has an idea of when this person arrived in Zoltan, but they need to identify them via Divine Blessing to narrow it down."

"Still, can something like that really be deduced with a blessing? There are plenty of people with the same blessings, and there are some who have not reported theirs to the holy church at all," Baron William responded.

"And that makes it possible for us to surmise who they're looking for as well," Ruti said, nodding. "It can't be a common blessing, and I don't believe it's one that'd go unreported, like Manslayer or Ripper, either. It must be a rarer, upper-tier blessing. The Champion, Sword Saint, Archmage, Hierophant, Crusader… Someone with a powerful blessing that isn't the sort you'd keep secret."

"I see…!"

Limiting the scope to those who'd come to Zoltan rather than natives would significantly narrow the list, too.

"Also, if possible, I'd like to meet Prince Salius directly to glean what I can. I suspect that he might not be acting as an official representative of Veronia."

"Why is that?"

"Right now, Veronia is isolated and separate from the rest of the continent. King Geizeric managed to make Veronia a world power in a single generation, but he's ninety years old now. The nobility and common citizens are uneasy about their nation's stance of neutrality toward the demon lord's armies. Making an enemy of the holy church could spark a major insurrection. Could there really be someone in Zoltan who's worth that tremendous risk? It's hard to believe Veronia would gamble by refusing to explain its actions."

"When you put it that way, it is certainly odd."

Mayor Tornado, Baron William, and the various guild heads listened intently to Ruti.

The young woman was by no means eloquent, but her words carried the experience of her many battles. Even without knowing her past, the dependability she exhibited removed the doubts of the assembled officials.

Typically, Ruti struggled when it came to communication, but in situations like this, there was no one more reliable.

Tisse was reminded of how incredible her friend was.

"I'd also like to see the official letter bearing Prince Salius's request to see whether it really has the seal of the Veronian royal family—"

"There isn't one," Baron William cut in.

Ruti went stiff for a moment. "What do you mean there isn't one?" she asked.

"Exactly what I said. Prince Salius made a verbal demand for the records. There's no mistaking that Prince Salius is who he claims to be, however. One of my subordinates was an adventurer before settling in Zoltan. He's seen Prince Salius before and confirmed his identity."

For the first time since arriving, Ruti looked a bit troubled. After taking a moment to consider, she replied, "I'll investigate concerning that point as well, then. In ten days' time, I'll report my progress, so please stall as best you can. Claim that the mayor is working to persuade the holy church. Bishop Shien, please gather together a list of all the things that the holy church wants to ask and have it sent to Mayor Tornado tomorrow. The guard should be on watch for the townspeople getting on edge and take care to prevent any rumors from spreading. Baron William, you should keep your knights at the ready and train them in evacuation procedures to ensure they can get the villagers out of town at a moment's notice in case the prince decides to attack. With the water routes blockaded, trade by land will become all the more crucial, so the guilds should seize the initiative and start preparing the necessary infrastructure."

"U-understood."

"That's something I can do! Leave it to me!"

The deadlocked council leaped into action at Ruti's words. Now that they knew what they should be doing, the various guild heads were no longer hesitant.

"Wow, I never would have guessed you to be so skilled in these sorts of matters, too. It'd be a weight off my shoulders to know that someone as capable as you might stand among Zoltan's leaders someday."

"Indeed. If you ever want to join the army, we would gladly welcome you immediately at the level of a squire. Or, if you would like, I can lend you some soldiers to reclaim the lands being held by the hill giant Dundach, and you can become a noble. I'd gladly endorse your request for a grant of peerage as the guardian of those lands."

Both Mayor Tornado and Baron William readily pitched their offers to Ruti. However…

"I don't need that. I have my herb farm."

She turned them both down without so much as a polite smile.

The two were silent for a moment before forcing grins to escape the awkward mood. Then they insisted that Ruti come to them should she need anything.

*　　*　　*

With the meeting over, Ruti and Tisse left.

"So then, where should we begin?" Tisse asked.

"I need a dose of big brother," Ruti responded bluntly.

"Huh?"

"It's been a long time since I had to endure a serious talk for so long, so I need more of him to recharge."

At first, Tisse thought Ruti was joking, but her face was deadly serious.

"W-well, you do need to get your sword, I suppose."

Tisse could not help breaking into a smile at seeing Ruti say something like that with such a genuine expression.

For the two of them to protect Zoltan, Ruti needed to see her brother, and so they did.

*　　*　　*

"So that's what was going on."

"Mhm."

I served up a couple of plates of tomato and cheese pasta I had thrown together with what was available while listening to Ruti.

"Sorry it's just leftovers."

Ruti and Tisse had been called to the meeting right as they were getting ready to break for lunch, so they hadn't had anything to eat yet.

Obviously, Ruti could reactivate her blessing's skills that gave her immunity to hunger and fatigue, but she elected not to.

After finishing off the pasta, she sighed contentedly.

"Your cooking is always so delicious."

Seeing her happy face, I broke into a smile, too.

"Happy to please."

My little sister had cleared her plate perfectly. Not even the tiniest bit of tomato remained. She looked pleased as she wiped her mouth with a handkerchief.

I started to clean up the dishes, but Tisse stopped me with a polite gesture.

"I'll take care of that," she said before standing up and gathering the tableware herself. "You and Rit should talk with Ms. Ruti."

"Got it. Thank you, Tisse."

"It seems like there's a bit going on under the surface with this incident," Tisse added before leaving to wash the dishes.

That was true. This could easily become the most significant incident since the founding of the Republic of Zoltan.

Hopefully, it would resolve peacefully before it got to that, however.

"What do you think, Big Brother?"

"Hmmm… I agree with your line of thought. Given that there isn't any official diplomatic message, it's hard to believe that Prince Salius is acting under the direction of the Kingdom of Veronia itself. He's threatening Zoltan even though Avalonia has recognized it as an independent state. With the war against the demon lord's forces, Avalonia won't go to war with Veronia to protect us, but there will be diplomatic upsets. Even if Prince Salius were the future king, it's incredibly risky to do something like this on his own."

"He's not even very high on the succession list, right?" Rit asked.

"Yeah. Prince Salius is the king's eldest son, but his mother, the king's first wife Queen Misphia, disappeared, so he dropped to third place. The children of the king's second wife Queen Leonor moved ahead of him. Prince Yuzuk is first, and Prince Silverio is second.

In Veronia, the primary successor inherited everything, with some land and wealth being allotted to the remaining brothers afterward. Given Salius had dropped in the order, Yuzuk could use his actions in Zoltan as an excuse to cut him out of any inheritance or provision," I replied.

"That's...pretty substantial. That would affect more than the prince; it'd destroy his allies as well."

"Whatever he's after must be important enough to gamble everything."

There was plenty I could guess at, but I'd never met Prince Salius before.

The Kingdom of Veronia had once been a potential enemy to the world. Even now, it remained neutral in the war with the demon lord's armies. During my time in Avalonia, all I ever heard of Veronia were biased claims based on peoples' disapproval of the other nation.

"If it were you, what would you do next, Big Brother?"

"Hrmmm." I thought a bit before continuing. "Well, going to Veronia to investigate would be the best, but..."

"With the airship, it would probably be half a month for a round trip," Ruti said.

My eyes went wide. "Wow! It's that fast? But the airship would draw too much attention."

"Mhm."

A one-way voyage would take over two months by sea. If airships were ever mass-produced, the world would change pretty dramatically.

"The holy church will need to share whatever they know regarding the current political situation in Veronia. We can likely entrust that task to Bishop Shien. Our goal should be deducing who Prince Salius is seeking," I stated.

"I've already asked Bishop Shien to look into any people with notable, rare blessings using the holy church's records," Ruti responded.

"All right, so let's focus on what you and Tisse can do, then."

"Mhm."

"At least one person in Zoltan already knows who Prince Salius is after."

"There is?" Tisse asked, having returned from cleaning up after our lunch.

I smiled. "Of course. The person he's searching for would know."

"I guess that's true..."

"No one in Zoltan knows what Prince Salius's goal in all this is. That's why we're all shocked and having discussions like this one," I explained. "However, if there were someone who was aware of the prince's aim, they'd have an entirely different reaction. It might be to hide or run away. See what I mean?"

"Ahh." Ruti nodded in comprehension. "So we should keep an eye out for any who are behaving differently."

"If it were me, that's probably how I'd start."

"Thanks, you really are reliable, Big Brother."

Ruti stood up and leaned over the table to hug me.

"Do you need any more help?" I asked.

"No, it's fine. You have your slow life."

My sister released me, and, with a smile, she grabbed the goblin blade she'd left in my shop.

"This is my slow life."

* * *

The next morning.

Riding one of the Zoltan navy's ships, Mayor Tornado headed out to the warship where Prince Salius was staying.

Calling it the "Zoltan navy" sounded nice, but the members were all sailors from trade and fishing vessels without any maritime combat experience. An unease was quickly settling over the boat as it approached the galley, and conversation died down.

"Can't blame them for getting nervous."

Mayor Tornado himself was doing his best to keep from being intimidated by the enormous warship that seemed to grow larger the nearer he got to it.

He knew little of boats and had to assume that the sailors, who were more knowledgeable on the subject, were dreading this even more than he was. They understood just how easily they would all be killed—how little they could do to resist—if the looming warship decided to go after them.

In truth, however, Veronia would be the side to regret any open hostility. For on the boat with Mayor Tornado was the Hero and one of humanity's strongest Assassins.

"It's reassuring to have the two of you accompanying me," Tornado admitted to the pair of women standing beside him. "Tifa and Miss Ru—Erm, I suppose I should go with Miss White Knight?"

"Mhm."

Tisse had her standard light armor, shortsword, and hidden throwing knives, but Ruti was wearing a different outfit than usual. Today she was clad in full plate armor and a helmet with a visor that concealed her face. Her chest plate bore a lion crest—the emblem used by masterless knights who traveled the lands in search of self-improvement and glory.

I've never been to Veronia, but the royalty of a major country might well know my face from somewhere.

Red had been wary of being targeted by the demon lord's army ever since he and Ruti had embarked on their quest, and he'd been careful that there were no pictures of his sister's face. Thus, despite Ruti's fame, only people who had met her in person knew what she looked like. It was quite unlikely that Prince Salius would recognize her, but Ruti had donned the armor just to be safe.

She and Tisse were accompanying Mayor Tornado under the guise of protection, but they also wanted to see Prince Salius for themselves and hear what he had to say. They still did not have enough information to negotiate with the prince, though, so this trip would only be for the purposes of sizing up the person whom they were dealing with. Neither Ruti nor Tisse had any intention of speaking during this meeting.

Finally, the little Zoltan sailing ship pulled up alongside the giant Veronian warship.

The galley's characteristic long oars loomed overhead, not unlike guillotines waiting to fall.

A ladder was lowered from above, and Mayor Tornado, Ruti, Tisse, and three soldiers climbed up to the warship's deck.

The Veronian sailors wore chain mail vests. It was light armor, but anything heavier would make it difficult for them to swim. They had daggers and long cutlasses at their waists, and bows and quivers on their backs. Each of them had a shabby shirt over their armor to keep it from getting hot from the sun.

They looked more like pirates than a true navy, or at least that was the impression Tisse had.

"Ahoy, my dear Zoltan friend. It's only been a day, hasn't it?"

A smiling, well-tanned man who looked to be in his late thirties appeared from the door into the ship. Ruti had heard that the prince should have been pushing fifty years old, though.

"Standing around on deck in winter is poison for the body. Please, come inside."

Standing three steps behind this man was a beautiful woman with silver hair gathered into a side ponytail. Her ears were long, and she wore an eyepatch over her right eye. Ruti could see a scar poking from above and below the bit of cloth.

"Lilinrala of the Elven Corsairs," Tisse murmured.

The strange band of pirates led by a high elf whose infamy had spread far.

Crueler than humans and unaffected by the passage of time, Lilinrala's fearsome deeds had earned her a place in legends the world over.

When Geizeric betrayed and overthrew the previous Veronian king, Lilinrala's crew had sided with him and destroyed the country's navy. After the battle, Lilinrala and her pirates became the new navy, and had served King Geizeric ever since. Their longevity meant that even though their liege was getting on in years, they were still hale, and sat at the heart of Veronia's government.

It's possible she's a body double, but that wound matches the stories of Lilinrala. Which means one of Geizeric's allies, the head of Veronia's entire maritime fleet, came all the way out to Zoltan… Why?

Tisse quietly explained about Lilinrala to Mayor Tornado, who blanched. In Zoltan, Tornado was considered able, skilled, and bold, but the current situation had pushed the man entirely beyond his limits. He started to pull back uneasily.

"It's okay," Ruti assured from behind her visor. "No matter who we're up against, our goal remains the same."

"R-right."

There was no hint of nervousness in Ruti's voice. Mayor Tornado took heart in that, and reassumed a demeanor befitting Zoltan's leader.

The Republic of Zoltan was nothing more than a city-state established on the frontier by pioneers. Still, it was an independent entity. There was no denying that Zoltan paled in comparison to Veronia's might, but Mayor Tornado could not be abasing himself before a prince.

"By all means, please lead the way." There was a tremble to his voice, but the mayor flashed a grin as he responded to Lilinrala.

Prince Salius, Lilinrala, and Mayor Tornado sat around a table.

There were two high elf guards behind the prince. The scars and burns on their handsome faces attested to the fact that they were experienced sailors who had survived more than their share of combat.

"So then, do you bring good news?"

There was a friendliness to the prince's tone, but also an arrogance in his gaze that was almost as if he were addressing a retainer. Tornado furrowed his brow ever so slightly in discomfort, but his smile did not slip.

"Unfortunately, the holy church is rather vehemently opposed. As you are undoubtedly aware, your request is unprecedented. I am currently in the process of persuading the bishop, and I believe the results will be to your liking, if you would be willing to give me just a little bit more time. The bishop surely recognizes the reality of the situation. He merely wishes to take all steps necessary to assert that he did his best to defend the holy church's prerogatives.

It won't be an issue. With just a little time, it will all be resolved. With regard to your highness's request, the upper levels of Zoltan are all in agreement that we should cooperate."

Having said that much, the mayor wiped away the sweat on his forehead with a handkerchief.

Partway through, the grin had vanished from the prince's face and he stared straight into Tornado's eyes without expression. The mayor of Zoltan felt a dull ache as his heart raced from the tension, but he bit his lip, refusing to show weakness.

"I see, so the holy church refused."

"I'm doing my best to persuade them."

"And you say you require more time."

The prince's tapping finger echoed through the room. It was clear from his expression that he was irritated. Ruti watched him in wonder.

There's no way he didn't anticipate opposition from the largest organization on the continent. As prince, he has been immersed in politics for decades now. Surely, he'd understand that much. This can't be more than a façade to increase the pressure.

Ruti was staring at the prince from behind her visor.

I don't get it…

She had always struggled with those sorts of things. When it came to working out what other people were thinking, she just could not seem to get the hang of it. Ruti screwed up her face in frustration.

Because of the Hero blessing, Ruti had grown up without knowing many human emotions, leaving her overwhelmingly inexperienced when it came to empathizing with others. This was why she had unintentionally intimidated Tisse so many times in the past. Her natural difference in mentality likely had something to do with it, too.

That quirk and the fact that she only had eyes for her older brother were why Red had handled all critical negotiations when they'd traveled together. Until recently, Ruti had not even realized that she was actually a terrible communicator.

It's fine, though, because Big Brother understands me.

Having quit being the Hero and settled down in Zoltan, Ruti had started to feel the need to better express herself. However, she was also glad that Red had no problem comprehending her, tempting her toward a turn for the worse. Ultimately, she decided to leave it all up to Tisse, this time.

Fine, fine, I've got it.

Tisse flashed a slightly troubled smile, as if to indicate she had known it would come to this and observed the prince in Ruti's stead.

It feels like he's impatient.

Salius looked on edge, even though he was clearly in the superior position. It wasn't as though he'd been unable to get his desires across; he'd done a fair job of pressuring Zoltan without doing so outright. By Tisse's assessment, he was by no means a master negotiator, but he certainly seemed as skilled as the average member of a royal family.

Which means that whoever he's searching for is just that important. It also suggests some kind of time limit.

All that, combined with what Red had mentioned the day before, was helping Tisse piece things together. The only thing that remained was to test whether her conclusion was correct.

...!

Just then, Tisse felt a chill down her spine.

Lilinrala was silently staring daggers at her.

That was a whole lot of bloodlust out of nowhere. I guess that's a former legendary pirate for you. No, maybe she still is a pirate?

Lilinrala's gaze felt less like the well-honed blade of a famed sword and more like that of a blood-drenched cutlass that had robbed untold people of their lives.

It's still nothing compared to when I first met Ms. Ruti, though.

A slight grin crossed Tisse's lips as she thought back on that. She quickly braced herself, but the discussion came to a close without incident.

No matter how impatient Prince Salius was, this was not a place where he could resort to force. The holy church's opposition was predictable, and the administrative forces in Zoltan were doing what they could. That was already more than conciliatory enough for the current stage of negotiations.

Lilinrala agreed with the mayor's idea of a two-week deferral before meeting again for further discussions, and though he seemed dissatisfied, the prince had accepted this as well.

For now, Zoltan had gained some time to search for whoever Salius was after, which was what Ruti had wanted.

As the Zoltan group climbed down the ladder back to their boat, a small shadow hopped down onto Tisse's back.

"Nice work."

Tisse thanked her little partner, who had been off investigating the ship on his own.

Mister Crawly Wawly waved both his front legs gently, as if to say, "It was nothing."

* * *

There was a sound of boots walking across the wooden floor.

Lilinrala was pacing slowly back and forth in the cabin.

"Who is that girl?"

Lilinrala bore the Divine Blessing of the Pirate and was a natural born buccaneer, taking to her blessing like a fish in water. She had acquired her own ship, formed the Elven Corsairs, and sailed all around Flamberge, Veronia, and Avalonia, building her fame and carving out many bloody legends in the process.

She was confident that her blessing level, forged in decades of battle, was second only to the Pirate King Geizeric's in all of Veronia. Her skill Strong Impression hit targets with an intense bloodlust that instilled terror and robbed them of their judgment.

No one in some backwater place like Zoltan should have maintained their composure in the face of her ability.

"But that girl… Not only did she keep her calm, she even smiled."

The discussion today had been the equivalent of testing their blades on each other. The young girl serving as the mayor's guard had faced Lilinrala's haughty strike and parried it deftly. Lilinrala was loath to admit that of an enemy, but it was true. There was a hint of frustration in her astonished sigh.

Lilinrala had only agreed to Zoltan's proposed two-week extension because she recognized that the situation would not be as easy to deal with as she'd first anticipated. She felt it necessary to investigate the heroes of Zoltan more closely and devise how best to deal with them.

"It was careless not to research what these people have been keeping here. As a pirate, I'm ashamed of myself." Lilinrala's face twisted into a ferocious expression she had not worn in years. "Fine, bring it on."

She began to rework her plan for raiding the town, considering her minions and the man she had hired.

Chapter 2

How to Catch a Kind High Elf

Three days had passed since the meeting with Prince Salius and Lilinrala.

"I'm back."

I had just gotten back to the shop after a meeting at the Merchants Guild.

Rit smiled. "Welcome back."

"The trading ships have all been wiped out, apparently."

They hadn't actually been attacked. However, all of them were avoiding Zoltan because of Lilinrala's warship.

Trade with Zoltan wasn't exactly a big profit driver to begin with. It was just a convenient place for traders to hawk whatever leftovers they had. A small profit like that wasn't worth risking your life.

"But Zoltan is basically self-sufficient, isn't it?" Rit took my coat and put it away.

"Yeah. Food, salt, clothes, firewood, and things like that will just be a little on the short side, and the upper crust won't be able to get any luxury items, but it won't have a big impact. But there's a problem."

"A problem?"

"With that huge boat out there, no one's going out to fish."

Even the hardy fishers who would challenge a sea monster armed with nothing but a harpoon were scared of the giant warship.

"Ahh, that. Yeah, your seafood stew is delicious. It's a shame not to be able to have that anymore!" Rit responded indignantly.

"When you combine that with the lack of trade ships, a big issue arises."

"Which is…?"

"Oil."

"Oh. Right." Rit nodded. "The oils used in Zoltan are either imported vegetable ones or those from fish caught at sea."

Zoltan exported sugar and imported olive oil and canola oil. Locals produced fish oil, but it had an unpleasant odor, which meant it didn't see much use in Zoltan. The surrounding villages bought it, however.

This meant the production base for fish oil was small, and there was little inventory. And because larger merchant ships didn't visit Zoltan very often, the imported vegetable oils generally came in smaller quantities. So the stock was low there, too.

All of Zoltan's oil reserves would run dry before long. That had been the biggest concern at the Merchants Guild meeting. The higher-ups had pleaded with everyone to do something, but the only thing that could be done was to buy up all of the oil, place it under guild management, and limit sale and distribution to ration what was left.

"An army fights on its stomach. When supplies run out, morale will follow quickly," I said.

"Yeah." Rit had experienced that much for herself during the siege of Loggervia. She knew firsthand just how much the lack of everyday necessities could make everyone uneasy. "So you won't be able to use oil in your cooking… At this rate, my spirits are going to hit rock bottom." Rit's expression looked grave.

Wait, that's *your problem?*

"Yeah, no cooking oil will definitely be an issue. It's a reminder of just how far we've come from eating nasty food every day."

"Also, that means no more soap, either, since oil is used to make that, too! And after I went to all that work for silky smooth skin for you!"

Oh. That's pretty bad.

"Ah, your face suddenly got really serious, Red."

"Is there anything we can do?" I wondered.

The two of us sat down next to each other and started thinking.

"In Loggervia, we made oil using olives."

"There aren't any olive trees around Zoltan, though."

"Figures. What about trade by land?"

"Oil is relatively cheap for its volume, so trade by land would be rough."

We bounced a few ideas off each other, but none of them really stuck.

"What about using the fat from monsters to make oil?" Rit suggested.

"Anyone who could fight monsters is busy right now protecting Zoltan."

A sudden reduction in the monster population came with its own problems. Other monsters would expand their territory to fill the gap, which might lead to even stronger monsters near Zoltan settlements.

"Yeah, I guess that's no good..."

I brought out some tea and cookies so that we could take our time to consider the issue. We both sipped pensively from our cups.

"Delicious," Rit remarked with a sigh. "Weren't these tea leaves imported, too?"

"It's a blend of foreign leaves and ones I gathered up on the mountain."

"Losing this would be awful. The tea goes so perfectly with sweet cookies." Rit caressed the cup.

"The price of sugar should drop at least."

"But that's just sugar... I'm the kind of person who prefers sweet food combined with a drink that isn't sweet," Rit pouted. "I know! Why don't you just create a recipe for making a new kind of oil!" After saying that, though, she collapsed onto the table. "I guess that's impossible."

But...

"I wouldn't go that far..."

"Wait, so you can?!" Rit suddenly sat up straight. "Is there anything my Red can't do?"

"No, I can't say for certain that I'd be able to do it."

I scratched the back of my head apologetically for getting Rit's hopes up.

"So which is it, then?"

"Zoltan's sugar is made using sap from coconut trees, right?" I said.

"Yeah. We used beets in Loggervia. I was surprised to find out you could use tree sap to make it."

"The villages that make the sugar also eat the coconuts, and I've heard they also make fishing nets from them, but that's about all, currently."

"Are you saying they can be used as a source of oil, too?"

"Yeah. It should be possible... At least I think so."

Zoltan had started as a pioneer town. It wasn't like anyone here was particularly well-versed in uses for coconuts. When it came to things like that, the locals weren't any more knowledgeable than your average person in Central. However, the people of the south seas allegedly considered the coconut to be a wondrous thing that could provide everything humans needed. A single coconut tree gave you water, food, cloth, rope, a ship, and oil—everything needed for sailing the seas.

"...Or so I've been told," I explained.

"That's amazing! If you knew that, you should have said something sooner."

"Don't get your hopes up. Remember, that's all I've got. I know that you *can* get oil from a coconut, but I don't really know the process, or if there's anything that needs to be added to make it work."

Rit slumped back in her chair a bit. "Ahhh, I see."

"I don't think there's much I'll be able to do this time," I admitted.

"Okay, I'll go to the Mages Guild and borrow some alchemy tools real quick!"

"Huh?"

"My Red truly is amazing!" Rit was in high spirits as she grabbed my hand. "If we know that much, all that's left is to experiment, right? I'll buy a bunch of coconuts, too."

She was right. If I didn't know the answer, we could just employ some trial and error.

Rit was always showing me the way forward.

"All right, let's give it a shot."

"Yeah!"

Rit dashed outside while I stayed behind to watch the shop.

Sales had been high the past few days because of the unease caused by the battleship, but everyone had already stocked up by now, so there weren't many customers today. I was just watching the store by myself.

Without Rit there, it was quiet and a bit lonely.

I spent my free time considering ways of getting oil from coconuts, but I couldn't bring myself to focus on the matter.

"Hmmm."

I didn't want to figure out how to make coconut oil so much as I hoped to find the answer with Rit.

"Hm, I've really gone soft."

I chuckled wryly to myself before setting that aside. Fighting and worrying were things for the city's higher-ups to deal with. I was just an apothecary.

My life with Rit was the most important thing to me.

* * *

"That's our Rit for you! Zoltan's hero, even in retirement!"

"To think there was a way to make oil like this! There's truly no substitute for the knowledge gained from traveling the world!"

"Please register with the Merchants Guild! We would love to have you as an honorary adviser!"

The traders crowded Rit, showering her with an avalanche of praise. I was standing outside the throng, clapping from the side.

We had experimented in the workroom for two days. At first we had tried just wringing the oil out like with olives, but that hadn't worked. When I'd begun wondering whether to try heating it, cooling it, melting it, drying it out, Rit had said, "Just do it all." She got so into it that she even used her Power of Bear enhancement magic.

Seeing her so fired up had motivated me, too, and we'd worked through the night, attempting everything we could think of. And fortunately, our efforts had yielded results.

"Take the coconut meat, smash it up, add a little bit of flame grass powder, leave it in a bucket for one hour, take the semisolids that rise to the surface, then put them into a pot and heat until they become a translucent oil. After that, all that's left is to strain away the dregs. There weren't any issues with the recipe. Our alchemists were able to follow the instructions without any issues," one of the merchants said as he looked at a document.

The Merchants Guild operated so smoothly, despite Zoltan's typical laziness, because of men like him, who were quick and eager.

"The only part that requires a skill is making the flame grass powder. Anyone can handle the actual oil production. There may even be a species of coconut that's better suited for making oil, removing the need for the flame grass," I remarked.

"Further improving the method is an intriguing proposition, but the very fact that coconut oil production is feasible is wonderful. To think it would be this simple to acquire what was a scarce resource..." The merchant nodded in marvel and then extended his hand with a smile. "Thank you very much, Red. Our guild is lucky to have someone like you in Zoltan."

* * *

There was a warmth in my heart that I hadn't felt in a while, and I couldn't help breaking out into a satisfied grin as Rit and I made our way back to the shop.

Despite having developed such a crucial new product, we'd admittedly sold off the method rather cheaply. With trade cut off, merchants were the ones hurting for income, not me. And we had been entrusted with the oil production and distribution; that would be enough.

Plus, as a reward for our contributions, the Merchants Guild had waived my member fees for five years, and the loan I had taken to get the shop open had been written off, too.

"I'm perfectly satisfied with this. You don't need to get so worked up about it."

"Hrmph." Rit looked miffed. "You were the amazing one, but all they did was praise me… I don't like it!"

"There were people who acknowledged me, too. It's fine."

"You should make more of a point of selling just how great you are sometimes!"

"The whole point of my coming here was not to stand out too much."

"But I want people to congratulate us together!"

So that was what was bothering Rit. She was upset that we weren't getting shared credit for what we had done as a pair.

"It makes me happy to see everyone holding you in such high esteem."

"I just wish they'd understand how amazing you really are!"

"Ah-ha-ha, sorry, sorry. You understanding is enough for me, though," I assured her.

"Ugh." Rit covered her mouth with her bandana as she glared at me. Her cheeks were turning a little bit red. "Saying stuff like that to make me happy is not fair."

Rit held out her hand, and I took it in mine.

"It's the truth, though," I replied.

"I know it is, but…argh." Rit smiled in resignation. "Fine, I'm going to keep fawning over you by myself."

She blushed after saying that, and we continued home, hand in hand.

*   *   *

It was nearing evening the next day, and Rit and I were working in the shop.

"Shall we call it a day a bit earlier today?" I asked when customers started to get few and far between.

"I don't mind. Did you have something to do?"

"I was thinking of going to meet Yarandrala to see if she had any advice about gathering coconuts."

Until now, Zoltan had only used the sap of coconut trees for making sugar. The villagers in nearby settlements either ate the coconuts or made nets from them. Making oil required a lot of the fruit, so I'd wanted to ask an expert on plants about how best to harvest them while being careful not to overdo it and run out.

"Oh yeah, she was coming by to hang out every day at first, but she hasn't stopped by since after the festival," Rit remarked.

"I had actually been wondering about that, too. Considering her personality, it seems weird she hasn't stopped by every day."

"Then let's get our work finished up quickly."

Rit started quickly checking over our sales. She was a practiced hand at that, so I left her to it. Back when she started, she'd been a lot more awkward.

We had met again near the end of summer, and we were pushing toward the end of winter now. Both of us had gotten much more comfortable with running an apothecary.

"I'm done over here."

"I'm almost finished, too."

And with that, work was complete for the day.

"Good job, Rit."

"You too, Red."

We double high-fived, then hugged each other and spun around.

"What are you going to do?" I asked.

"I'm coming with, obviously. Yarandrala's a friend, after all. I'm going to change real quick, so just wait a minute." Rit grinned and then dashed over to the bedroom.

* * *

For a small place like Zoltan, the harbor district was the one window to foreign lands.

"There are a lot of ships."

It wasn't that there'd been a sudden rush of arrivals. Rather, all the vessels that would typically be out fishing were still docked.

"I guess trade and fishing really are going to be a problem."

"Zoltan's never seen such a big warship before, after all," Rit responded.

We couldn't see it from where we were walking, but if we took a ship out into the water just a little bit farther toward the river, the Veronia galley would surely be there.

It was an old-style design from eighty years ago, but it was still a combat-ready powerful sea vessel. It was on a whole other level from the small modified merchant ships that pirates around these parts used.

"Even if they haven't come to declare war, they could easily capture or sink any Zoltan vessels if they felt like it. Anyone would feel uneasy with that thing nearby."

After a short stroll, we heard the drunken singing of jobless sailors hanging out at a bar. They weren't very good, but it made for fair enough background noise as Rit and I walked. The red sun setting over the river was lovely, and despite the recent trouble, it still felt like a peaceful scene.

The inn where Yarandrala was staying was on the other side of the tavern where the sailors had gathered.

"It's the first time I've been around here," I commented.

I was a little bit surprised by how quiet it was. As if the usual boisterous harbor bustle had all been a lie.

A small creek burbled, and the trees rustled. It was almost like a little park. There were three lodges lined up there.

"This is housing for spirit users," Rit explained. "It's pretty common for people with blessings that let them sense spirits of the sea or storm to become sailors."

"That's right, there was someone with a Wind Druid blessing who was a privateer captain back in the capital."

As I recalled, he'd been a slender guy, and he said his hobby was playing a lyre in the forest for the songbirds on his days off. But that delicate-looking man was a commodore at the head of a fleet of forty large corsairs. According to one of the crew, he was merciless and cruel out on the seas, and had no qualms about ordering someone to go to a nearby village to kidnap people to make up for a shortfall in crew.

I never dealt with him that much, but the army had viewed his cruelty as a problem.

Rit had a comfortable smile on her face as she looked around, perhaps because of her Spirit Scout blessing.

Evidently, the forest had been maintained here so spirit users could be at ease.

I walked through the trees and opened the door of a lodge that felt like a little cabin in the middle of the woods.

* * *

"I can't believe she wasn't there," Rit said. "Yarandrala moved without even telling us."

Rit and I were resting under a tree, eating some apples we had gotten at the inn. They were crunchy, with a nice texture and a delicious mix of sweet and sour.

Yarandrala was nowhere to be found. Apparently, she had moved out the day after the festival. The woman running the lodge didn't know where she had gone.

Rit tossed an apple core into the trash. "What should we do?"

"I was thinking of going looking for her," I responded, tossing my core into the trash as well.

It was strange for Yarandrala to vanish without so much as a word.

"Did she get dragged into something?" Rit wondered aloud.

I thought for a moment before responding.

"That seems unlikely. If she had, I'm pretty sure she would have come to tell us."

"Maybe she just didn't get a chance to."

"With her abilities, even if she couldn't meet us in person, she'd find a way to let us know."

Yarandrala's blessing was Singer of the Trees. She could communicate with plants. From the timbers around us all the way to the nameless blades of grass on the side of the road, they could all be Yarandrala's messengers. That was how powerful her ability was.

"Maybe she stuck her nose into something she ought not to have," I suggested.

"Even so, she would tell us she was moving," Rit answered.

"Yeah, she'd definitely make a point of letting us know and telling us not to worry, but…"

"But…?"

"Well, suppose this was a personal matter. In that case, I bet she'd rather keep it quiet and solve everything on her own so as not to trouble us."

"Aww." Rit grimaced slightly, and then murmured, "I would have preferred if she talked to us about it."

"Me too. But either way, I was thinking of going to look for her. Whether we end up helping out or not is one thing, but we can provide emotional support, at least."

"I can understand not wanting to trouble friends, but I do worry about her. And I want to see her again."

"Yeah. Want to look for her together?" I suggested.

"Do we have any idea where to start?"

"Hmmm… Nothing but asking around blindly."

If Yarandrala had left the lodge while making a point not to leave any tracks, even Rit, with her Spirit Scout blessing, wouldn't be able to track her. My Guide wouldn't be any use, obviously.

"Fortunately, she has only been in Zoltan a little while, and she doesn't have many acquaintances here."

"True, that's probably a good place to start."

"All right… Why don't we start by paying Mogrim a visit."

I stood up, getting ready to head over to the blacksmith's shop back in our neighborhood.

Before we could leave, three men approached us. One of them caught my eye in particular. He had savage, drake-like eyes.

"Evening."

The drake-eyed man glared at me before nodding slightly and walking by. He and the other two headed toward the building we'd just left.

"Rit, what do you say we rest here a little longer?"

"That's fine with me… Who are they?"

The suspicious group opened the door to the lodging and went inside.

"They have high-level Assassin blessings. Each is probably over level 40."

"Assassins over level 40?! That's way stronger than Albert or Galatine!" Rit kept her voice low, but she couldn't hide her surprise.

"They definitely aren't from Zoltan. Probably came in from the outside."

"From the Assassins Guild?" Rit questioned.

"People with Assassin blessings were typically recruited into the guild, but that's not the case for all of them, so it's difficult to say," I answered.

"I guess so. Hmm… Do you think they've got something to do with the Veronian galley?"

"Hard to say without knowing more, but the arrival of an imposing ship and three people with high-level blessings so close together is too strange not to think they're connected."

"We can't forget that those three are searching the place where Yarandrala was staying," Rit reminded me.

"It might all be connected. Anyway, it doesn't seem like they've come to cause a fuss at least…"

I was watching carefully, but there didn't seem to be any sign of a fight in the lodge. The rough-looking trio appeared to be talking peaceably. I'd opted to stay and watch in case violence broke out, but fortunately, it seemed to be wasted effort.

"Looks like they are leaving," Rit whispered as she held out her hand.

I took it, and we walked out of the small grove together, playing the part of lovers coming to enjoy the forest scene. Well, it wasn't exactly an act, so we pulled it off quite naturally.

* * *

Rit and I could have tried speaking to the three, but without understanding the situation, it was too risky. For now, our best option was checking with the people who knew Yarandrala.

Thus, we made our way to Mogrim's shop.

"If it ain't Red and Rit. Come on in."

Mogrim was sitting at the counter. He broke into a smile when he saw us.

It was outside business hours, but still during the time when Mogrim stayed around in case someone needed something sharpened or the like. His customers weren't exclusively adventurers and soldiers. Mogrim also helped lots of carpenters and crafters who came to get their tools mended after work was finished.

"What brings you here? Did your sword break again?"

"Saying it like that makes it sound like I'm always destroying it! I was just wondering if Yarandrala had stopped by recently," I replied.

"Hm? That stubborn elf, huh?" Mogrim grimaced in disgust. I had thought they had maybe started to get along a bit after traveling together, but high elves and dwarves really did go together like oil and water. "As if that high elf would ever come 'round to see me!"

"What makes high elves so bad? Dwarves don't seem to have any issues with half-elves," I said.

"Half-elves don't have the same disgusting arrogance and irritating irresponsibility. They're practically the same as humans."

True. On a personality level, half-elves tended to be no different from humans. The vast majority of elves in Zoltan were half-elves, so I hadn't ever heard of them having issues with the local dwarves. The few high elves living in Zoltan probably didn't use the dwarf-run smithies.

Gonz looked the handsome elf, but he was just your average middle-aged guy on the inside.

"Okay, so she hasn't come by, then..."

"Aye, she hasn't… But…" Mogrim muttered, as if suddenly remembering something. "Godwin mentioned he had spoken with Yarandrala and Mistorm at the Adventurers Guild."

"Godwin and Mistorm?"

And just like that, two more names from Yarandrala's small pool of acquaintances popped up.

* * *

"All right, you better not oversleep tomorrow, you guys!" Godwin said.

"Got it!" Three tough-looking laborers nodded vigorously.

Evidently, they were preparing to leave when Rit and I arrived.

"Sorry to keep you waiting," Godwin apologized.

"Don't worry about it. Apologies for coming by all of a sudden while you were working."

"It's no problem at all."

Godwin smiled, not looking bothered at all. I couldn't help but smile to see him like that.

"Already getting ready for your trade route?" I inquired.

"Yep."

We were at a warehouse on the north side of Zoltan.

Godwin had been working into the night packing a horse-drawn cart full with bags of glass. The trade between Zoltan, the zoog village, and the gem giants was gearing up.

"I was worried you wouldn't be able to get together enough guards, what with the situation with Veronian galley and all," I said.

"Actually, more than half of the adventurers who were supposed to help me had to pull out, and I had to rush around some to keep everything together. I ended up contacting some old friends in the Thieves Guild who were on the outs lately and managed to recruit a few of them."

"The remnants of Bighawk's group? Can you trust them?"

"They're all real pieces of work without any moral code, but so long as I pay them, it'll be fine. They can tell as well as I can that they no longer have a future in the Thieves Guild. Working for me is a much better deal."

Godwin looked far more energetic and lively than when he'd been under Bighawk's thumb. Given Godwin's personality, I doubt he felt guilty working for the Thieves Guild, but something had happened recently that changed his values.

"Anyway, we wanted to ask you about Yarandrala and Mistorm," Rit began. "We're looking for Yarandrala and heard you had her and Mistorm at the Adventurers Guild recently. Could you tell us what you know?"

Godwin cocked his head to one side. "Wait, so now you guys are looking for her? Wasn't she the one looking for you just the other day?"

"Yarandrala moved without telling us. We were thinking that maybe she's been caught up in something unpleasant."

"Can't think of any trouble in Zoltan that'd be too much of a problem for her. There's that whole Veronian warship, but I've been busy getting ready for my trip, so I don't know much about that."

"Ruti, Tisse, and Mister Crawly Wawly are investigating that one."

"Well, if they're on it, then there's nothing to worry about!" Godwin flashed a relieved grin. "Honestly, I only just caught a glimpse of Yarandrala at the Adventurers Guild."

"Is there anything you can remember? Anything at all?" I implored.

"I saw her the morning after the festival. But it wasn't in the hall area of the guild where adventurers hang out. I went there to see about hiring a few people for my business. Master Mistorm put in a good word for me, so I had a meeting with Harold, Galatine, and Kevin, the second in command of the Zoltan guard. Pretty sweet how three of the big hitters were there for my meeting, huh? Heh-heh. Anyway, our meeting was in one of the guild's office rooms, though all that talk ended up being pointless in the end."

"And that was where you saw Mistorm?" I questioned.

"Yeah," Godwin replied. " Around when things were mostly hammered out, a worker rushed in looking flustered. He said that Master Mistorm had arrived. The report was really only for Harold and Galatine, but everyone in the room heard. After that, the two of them got up and left."

"That was still during the morning?"

"Yeah. I didn't have a clock around to say for sure, but I'd bet it wasn't even ten yet."

Rit and I had gone fishing the day after the festival. We had spotted the Veronian galley that afternoon. Prince Salius had apparently made contact the next day. Word of a giant warship approaching Zoltan was surely cause for Zoltan's bigwigs to call an emergency meeting. They probably would've rescheduled Godwin's trade meeting had they known about the galley already, so word couldn't have spread until later in the morning at the earliest.

"Anyway, since I owed my whole business to Master Mistorm, I figured I should make a point of saying thanks, so I left with Harold and Galatine, too. Then everyone else started following suit, hoping to speak with Master Mistorm. Galatine got really pissed." Godwin grinned as he recalled the scene. "Let me tell you, even Kevin cowered a little beneath his gaze. Anyway, I used that opening to hurry Harold out of the room and headed over to see Master Mistorm."

"I see."

"Yarandrala was with Master Mistorm when I found her, which was a bit of a surprise. Honestly, that elf scares me a little, so I hesitated for a moment. Then Galatine ran over and had a quick chat with Master Mistorm. Yarandrala and the two of them ended up heading out somewhere together."

"Mistorm, Yarandrala, and Galatine?"

Apparently, the Adventurers Guild was involved, or Galatine himself, at least.

"I guess the Adventurers Guild is our next stop, then," I stated.

"Ah, wait a sec," Godwin called. "If Tisse and Mister Crawly Wawly are getting involved with the Veronia thing, then could you pass on a message for me?"

"What is it?"

"I heard a bit of unpleasant news while rounding up some of my old Thieves Guild buddies."

"Oh?"

"There's rumors that some of the Zoltan bigwigs who think we should give in to Veronia have been gathering all the ruffians who worked for Bighawk."

"Assembling thieves, huh?"

"I know Mister Crawly Wawly can handle himself, but just to be safe, could you let him and Tisse know for me?"

I guess Godwin was worried about them. He really had changed.

* * *

Northern Zoltan was primarily expansive farm plots.

The northern district was the largest one, but there were few people living there. Most of the land was just fields for vegetables and wheat. Ruti's herb farm was on some land she and Tisse were renting up in that area.

Part of the reason the Adventurers Guild was in the northern district was because there were so many requests for dealing with agriculture-related issues. Zoltan's walls were more like a suggestion—fences that could easily be jumped. The guild had been placed in the North so it could respond to monsters and animals that hopped the wall and went after crops and farmers.

Perhaps the storms that rolled through made it difficult for the monster population to grow. Whatever the reason, the average level of monsters around Zoltan was pretty low. They grew in strength through survival of the fittest battles with other creatures. Monsters were born with sturdy bodies and powerful special abilities, and their levels rose based on how many living things they killed. However, in areas where natural disasters culled the local fauna population, you either wound up with an immensely mighty individual creature capable of overpowering whatever the world threw at it or got what Zoltan had—a relatively peaceful region where monsters barely survived hurricanes and the like.

Since Zoltan was so tranquil, the real reason the Adventurers Guild was up on the north side might well have been so it would be easier to hire additional help when farms were busy.

"Oh, if it isn't Miss Rit! It's been a while!" the woman at the counter called out excitedly.

"Hi, Louise. How have you been?"

"I've been good! But ever since you retired, we've been struggling with getting people to take more difficult quests. Mr. Bui disappears regularly and for long periods, and Ms. Ruhr and Ms. Tifa are more focused on agriculture, so they don't take the more involved jobs."

"I'm sorry."

"Ah, no, I'm sorry for bothering you with my complaints. This is just the norm. You were kind of the exception."

Louise had a heated look in her eyes as she looked at Rit. She must have been a fan of Rit the hero.

"Oh, so what brings you by today, Miss Rit?" Suddenly remembering herself, Louise's face turned red.

"I was hoping to meet with Galatine. Is he here now?"

"I'm incredibly sorry, but Mr. Galatine has gone to the cathedral."

"The cathedral. Bishop Shien's?"

"Yes, ma'am."

Had he gone there for a meeting about Prince Salius?

No, more importantly… Maybe…

I was standing behind Rit and sinking deep in thought. Louise leaned forward with a knowing look on her face.

"Are you perhaps looking for him about a quest to deal with the Veronian warship?"

"Hm? No, no. I'm just trying to find a friend."

"I see… It would have been reassuring to have Rit the hero on the case." Louise's shoulders slumped in disappointment.

"Sorry. However, if Ruti needs us, Red and I will be there to help."

Louise's face suddenly brightened. "Thank goodness! I was honestly really worried. Pirate King Geizeric is infamous, even here in Zoltan. Just imagining what sort of scary people might be on that ship… But with Ms. Ruhr, Ms. Tifa, Rit the hero, Mr. Galatine, and the rest of the old B-rank party, I'm sure we can overcome whatever danger might come our way!"

Rit blushed at Louise's excited volume.

"Did you say Galatine and the rest of the old B-rank party?" I asked.

"Ah, Mr. Red, the man who stole Miss Rit away from us."

"Huh? Uh, I guess… Umm, so does that mean Galatine and his companions are assuming the role of adventurers for the situation?"

"Hm? Ah, yes! He's left the guild matters to Harold. Mr. Galatine, Bishop Shien, Captain Moen, and Master Mistorm have reunited! It's a secret, apparently, but I'm sure it would be okay to tell you, Miss Rit!"

"Mistorm, too?"

She was old and retired, but Rit and I both knew that her strength made her Zoltan's most powerful mage. It made sense that Zoltan's retired heroes would rise up in the town's time of need, but…

Rit and I glanced at each other.

"It doesn't really make sense."

"Yeah."

* * *

It had started getting dark, and the sun was almost past the horizon.

Rit and I were walking together along a street in the central district.

"What do you think about Mistorm coming back as an adventurer?" Rit asked.

"A hero doesn't depart to save their homeland covertly. They raise their sword and move in the open to make it clear to all that they are taking action, like how Ruti attended the assembly. Becoming a pillar of support for your allies: That's what a champion of the people does. Whatever Mistorm's doing, if it's something she has to keep under wraps, then it feels like there's some ulterior motive."

"True."

Rit was a hero who had saved her country. She understood precisely what sort of role she had filled then far better than I did.

"You know...," I muttered as we walked along the well-kept road. "Wandering all around looking for something brings back memories."

"Memories?"

"From when I was traveling with Ruti. I did this a lot back then, going from place to place, following leads, tracking down information."

The Hero's journey hadn't been all glorious battles. Particularly at the outset, a lot of people laughed off the very existence of the Hero. Ruti and I had to earn trust by resolving local issues. Occasionally, the demon lord's forces sent in spies to disrupt humanity's alliance against them.

Our party was specialized for battle, so when it came to gathering information, our only choice was to do so head-on, from the ground up.

"After Yarandrala joined, we did things a little more like a proper Hero's party. We'd solve mysteries quickly by talking to plants and other amazing things like that," I explained.

Rit's expression turned wistful. "Right, you mentioned that investigation wasn't your forte in Loggervia."

Ah, back when we were investigating the mountain village.

"I'd like to have some of that preserved food you made back then again."

"Maybe I'll make some more again."

Rit smiled nostalgically.

"Loggervia was tough, but it was far from the worst we went through. At least you acknowledged Ruti's strength, Rit, even if you and your people wanted to protect your nation alone. When we were just starting out in Avalonia, local lords would openly decry Ruti as a false hero who'd tricked the king."

"Ugh, that sounds rough."

"It really got me down. Ruti never wanted to be the Hero, and she was still called a liar by those she fought to protect." My voice grew softer as memories of the old days surfaced in my mind. "I felt bad that she had to endure all that."

"It wasn't that bad."

"Ruti?!"

My sister had appeared out of nowhere and leaped into my arms. Although flustered, I caught her nonetheless.

"I don't mind what other people say about me. Back then, I was happy that you got mad at them for my sake. Those recollections are precious to me." Ruti gave me a big hug and smiled. "Thank you, Big Brother."

"It was my pleasure. If it was a nice memory for you, then that's enough for me."

"That makes me even happier."

Ruti squeezed me one more time and then reluctantly let go.

"What are you doing around here?" I questioned.

"Looking for Moen. I heard he was at the cathedral, so I was heading there."

"I see… Rit and I are actually searching for Yarandrala."

"Yarandrala?" Ruti parroted.

I explained what had happened.

"Ah, so then we're all going to the same place."

"If Moen is there as well, then maybe what we heard about the old B-rank party getting back together is true," I remarked.

Rit furrowed her brow. "It's unnatural for both Galatine and Moen to be out of contact during an emergency situation like this."

"True. And they were both against giving in to Veronia. It doesn't make sense that they would leave their leadership positions to take up arms."

"Speaking of," Rit said, looking around before her gaze landed on Ruti. "Is Tisse not with you?"

"I asked her to go to the Thieves Guild to ask for some help looking for any Veronian spies who may have already infiltrated Zoltan. Also, to make sure they know not to get too ahead of themselves and cause problems for anyone who actually is unrelated."

"That's my sister for you."

"Yay. Big Brother praised me."

Rit and I smiled at Ruti's blushing, though most people wouldn't have noticed her change in expression. Ruti seemed to be enjoying her freedom of emotion.

Smiling, flushing, getting angry on occasion, and smiling again.

Ruti was growing into a cute young woman.

* * *

The cathedral in the central part of Zoltan.

We passed through the imposing arch doorway of the cathedral in central Zoltan. Ahead, one of the local priests was speaking to a group of anxious townsfolk.

A young monk softly called out to us upon noticing our arrival. "If it isn't Ms. Ruhr and Miss Rit. Oh, and Mr. Red as well. Have you all come to offer a prayer to Lord Demis?"

"No, we heard Moen and Galatine were here."

"Ah, I see. Very well, I'll show you in."

The monk bowed slightly and led us to a door on the left. Rit looked a little bit uneasy.

"This works out fine for us, but should he really be doing this? Is it okay not to let them know we're here?" she asked.

"It's standard practice for the Zoltan holy church not to reject anyone who enters, so I guess there isn't a habit of asking Bishop Shien or Galatine whether it's okay. If they get annoyed at the monk, we can cover for him," I replied.

"Hmm… Okay."

We left the main nave, crossed a courtyard, took a passage into a small monastery area where the monks went about daily routines, and finally entered the holy church's office building, where the meeting rooms and such were located.

Unlike the cathedral, which had been an expensive project built by an architect and craftsmen called in from Central, this building had been designed by Gonz's great-grandfather. Thus, it resembled most other Zoltan edifices.

We followed the monk two doors down from the primary conference room. Then he knocked on a thick, sturdy oak door.

"Bishop, Ms. Ruhr, Miss Rit, and Mr. Red have come to see you."

I could sense a disturbance in the chamber. Unsurprisingly, it seemed like those inside were taken aback by our unexpected visit.

"…Really? Please, let them in," a voice called out from inside.

The young monk opened the door with both hands.

It was a small, windowless room. A plain round table stood in the center, encircled by four chairs. There was also a small altar and mat for meditation. Magic potions sat on a shelf pushed up against the wall, and both weapons and tools for maintaining them had been placed in a corner.

Looking to the side, I saw a lead sheet on the back of the door. I assumed the same material lined the interior of the walls. It was a countermeasure against abilities that made it possible to peer through solid objects and divination techniques.

"I see, so this is your old headquarters," I remarked.

Galatine nodded. "Indeed. It's been a while since we've used it, but I clean it every day, so it shouldn't be too musty."

"It does look well-kept. Though I imagine it gets hot in summer," replied Bishop Shien.

"Hah-hah-hah. Moen always complained about that."

"Can we save the stories from when I was an impertinent brat for later? Or never?"

Moen smiled awkwardly at Bishop Shien's teasing. Galatine was sitting at the table with them.

The conversation was congenial, but there was a sharpness in the trio's eyes. They couldn't mask the uneasy air now that a group of uninvited guests had come by.

"I'll excuse myself now." The young monk smiled and bowed before heading back, seemingly unaware of the discomfort.

Bishop Shien sighed.

"Please don't be upset with him. Given that Rit and Ruti are with me, I'm sure he thought we'd been called here for your meeting," I said.

"His ignorance is my failure as his teacher. His mistake will be corrected, but I won't scold him just to make myself feel better." Bishop Shien smiled gently. "Welcome to our old haunt. It's a pleasure to host the current generation's heroes."

Rit shrugged slightly at the greeting. "There's no reason for us to be walking on pins and needles around each other. We're all just Zoltan adventurers here, right?"

"True enough. We all share the same goal, after all. So then what brings you here today?" Bishop Shien questioned.

"I came to discuss guard deployment and to devise plans for training maneuvers," Ruti answered, looking over at Moen.

"I see. Well, I left my second-in-command, Kevin, in charge of those things…"

"Kevin isn't ready. He still lacks knowledge and experience. You should be leading the guards yourself."

"Kevin has had plenty of training…"

"It isn't enough." Ruti fixed Moen with a stiff gaze. The man was quickly overwhelmed by it, and his agitation became apparent. "It's more than that, however. Kevin is uneasy because you have left your post amid this unprecedented crisis. It's not just him, either. All of the guards are on edge. The loss in morale is dramatic."

"I—I see…"

Unable to provide an adequate response alone, Moen looked to Galatine and Shien for support. Galatine grimaced as he nodded.

"Ruhr is right. You may be the youngest of us, Moen, but you're the head of your organization. The captain of the guard is a cornerstone of Zoltan's defenses. We're just going to have to do this without you, I'm afraid."

"Wh-?! Wait just a minute, Galatine!" Moen frantically tried to argue.

Seeing that confirmed what I'd been suspecting.

"So the one Prince Salius is after is Mistorm."

At my statement, the three men's expressions shifted.

Seeing Galatine's fists clench, Rit took a half-step back, dropping into a stance where she could use her legs at a moment's notice if needed. Galatine's reaction was tantamount to admitting I was right.

This time, it was Moen who sighed.

"Wait, Galatine. Should a leader of the Adventurers Guild really get into a fight with one of his adventurers?"

We had gotten close with Moen after the incident with Ademi, so while he was on guard, he did not show any hostility. He seemed intent on keeping things civil. Naturally, I hoped for the same.

"Why do you believe that Prince Salius is searching for Mistorm?" Shien inquired, eyeing me closely.

"Moen would only leave his post for his family or his old comrades."

"I see." Shien smiled with resignation. "Red, I've heard about you from Galatine and Moen, and Mistorm as well. They've suggested that there's something about you that stacks up even when compared to Rit the hero or Ruhr. It looks like I have no choice but to agree with them."

"Sorry for putting you all on guard," I apologized. "Rit and I are only here because we're looking for our friend, Yarandrala."

Shien raised an eyebrow. "Ms. Yarandrala?"

"It sounds like you've met her before, then," I said.

"We only first spoke with her yesterday. I see… So that's what led you here."

"It was never our intention to get involved in your affairs. We owe Mistorm a debt, after all," I assured.

"You all went to the Wall at the End of the World together, right? Hearing about it after she got back was quite the shock. I'd thought she'd retired long ago, yet she trotted off on some perilous journey," Shien responded. Then his voice dropped low. "Honestly, she should have asked her old friends to come with."

"She was always like that, though," Galatine added, breaking into a smile.

It was clear that these old adventurers cared deeply for their friend. I'm sure Yarandrala would have appreciated their feelings toward Mistorm if she were there—I certainly did.

"At the very least, I can promise you we don't betray Mistorm," I stated.

"You have my thanks. Hearing that is enough for me," Shien said. Then he glanced over at Galatine and Moen. The two of them nodded.

I breathed a sigh of relief.

These were Mistorm's comrades, heroes who had protected Zoltan throughout the years. I was glad we'd settled things without making enemies of them.

* * *

Long before Albert came to Zoltan, a different B-rank adventurer party protected the city. Led by Mistorm, this group fought for decades, resolving many issues plaguing the region.

At first, there had only been three members. Moen joined later on, bringing the total up to four.

Mistorm the Archmage.

Galatine the Fighter.

Shien the Cleric.

Moen the Armored Knight.

Mistorm, in particular, had a powerful Divine Blessing that was rarely seen in Zoltan, and was subsequently incredibly popular.

When she was still active, she had even been hailed as Mistorm the Guardian of Zoltan.

Incidentally, Galatine was known as Galatine the Goblin Calamity; Shien had been Shien the Holy Wall; and Moen was referred to as Big Suit Moen.

Apparently, Moen disliked his less-than-spectacular nickname and complained about it sadly whenever it was mentioned.

These four were Zoltan's heroes. Curiously, there were no stories of Mistorm before she became an adventurer. People knew how Galatine had been bullied for being small as a child, and that his parents had made sure that he never went without food, even though they were poor. Moen was the illegitimate son of a Zoltan aristocrat who left home and entered the guard.

But there was nothing about Mistorm.

Her name only appeared the moment she formed a party with Galatine and Shien.

"It all started with the great panic caused by Goblin King Mulgarga fifty-one years back. The remnants of his crew attacked Zoltan forty-five years ago. Just when things were looking grim, a beautiful Archmage appeared. She was a champion who rallied the frightened people and led them to finally crush the remnants of the goblin army. There are no records or rumors from before that, though," I said.

"Because people in Zoltan don't pester others about their pasts. I'm sure there aren't many people who have inquired about yours either, Red."

"True enough. And I don't have any intention of prying into Mistorm's history, either. Rit and I are only trying to locate Yarandrala. But Ruti is the one tasked with resolving the current problem. Doesn't she at least deserve to know more?"

"I can understand how you feel. But even if we are her old comrades—in fact precisely because we are her old comrades—we can't expose her secrets."

I nodded. "Yeah, I can understand that stance. That's why I'd like you to tell us where Yarandrala is first. Is she with Mistorm?"

"Yes… Ordinarily, we'd be by her side, protecting her, but we've grown old enough now that we can't just abandon everything to fight for our friend… We're grateful to Yarandrala for her help."

"So then, where is she?" I pressed.

Shien pulled a map of the area around Zoltan down from a shelf and spread it across the table. It was far more precise than the ones being sold to the public.

"Yarandrala and Mistorm are in a village in the forest," he said.

"The woods, huh?"

"A group of assassins attacked Mistorm and Yarandrala saved her. For anything more, you should ask Yarandrala herself."

"Assassins… Okay, I understand. Thank you for trusting us," I replied.

Someone whom Mistorm would need help against… It has to be those three from the docks.

"As for the woods, Galatine and Moen can't really leave Zoltan, so I'll guide you," Shien stated.

"That would be best," Ruti agreed. "The guards need Moen to maintain the chain of command. And Harold, the head of the Adventurers Guild, believes that Zoltan should give in to Prince Salius's demands. Without Galatine around, the guild might switch sides."

Galatine looked frustrated at that remark. In terms of accomplishments and ability, he definitely outstripped Harold, but this was

Zoltan. Harold was older, so until he retired, Galatine would never run the Adventurers Guild.

"Ruhr's right. Shien, I'll leave Mistorm to you," Galatine said.

"You can count on me."

Despite Shien's reassuring response, Galatine and Moen looked vexed at not being able to rush to their comrade's aid.

Interlude

Youth 45 Years Ago

Goblin King Mulgarga, who had united goblins across the continent, had been defeated by the Bahamut Knights, but remnants of his forces still rampaged across the land.

After being bested by the Kingdom of Avalonia's army, the goblins fled to the frontier lands.

Peaceful Zoltan was no exception, and waves of the monsters poured in, leading to a spike in banditry and the most perilous era in Zoltan's history.

Two adventurers, a young Galatine and Shien, were facing off against more than a dozen of the creatures.

"Shien! Where are the guards?!" Galatine shouted.

The goblins were armed with spears, swords, and bows and wearing helmets. They were clearly stronger than the typical ones found in Zoltan. They had raised their blessings' levels through years of war and pillaging and were already strong enough that C-rankers like Galatine and Shien were having difficulty dealing with them.

"Hyah-hahhh!!!" the goblins cried as they charged.

Galatine swung his war hammer, smashing the head of the first to draw near. He hit the second with the gauntlet on his left hand. The third was done in by a blow to the jaw from his hammer. Unfortunately, a spear-wielding goblin managed to flank Galatine.

Fear of death rooted the man in place as the deadly weapon lanced for his side.

"Dimension Whip!"

Galatine's body quivered and vanished, only to appear again ten meters away.

"Heed my mantra! Wind of righteous destruction and revelation! Tornado Cutter!"

Shien hurled a blast of sharp wind, sending the goblins back. Using that opening, he grabbed Galatine's hand.

"We should retreat!"

"Ngh!"

The pair were only up against a single squad of goblins. Zoltan hardly possessed the most accurate data, but by recent calculation, there were at least one hundred of the monsters lurking about. It was hardly the time for Galatine and Shien to be taking risks.

"Our home… They're going to…!"

Zoltan had never seen this kind of threat before. It was supposed to be a peaceful, laid-back, boring place. Galatine was trembling with rage.

Even if they were only the remnants of a once-mighty army, these goblin soldiers had battled Central's Bahamut Knights. Fighters raised in Zoltan's tranquil lands stood no chance.

A previous B-rank party had already fallen to the monsters, and from the moment the goblins hoisted the party leader's head as a battle flag, Zoltan was as good as dead. Surrounding settlements were constantly being assaulted, but Zoltan's forces made no effort to help. People were too scared.

"Galatine. There are no reinforcements coming."

"Why not?! Elite or not, there are only one hundred of them! Zoltan is going to fall to a few dozen goblins?!"

"They fought in some of the major battles of our time and survived. We're just bit players who won't make the footnotes in the history books…"

Galatine and Shien had left home filled with youthful passion, planning to gather up the warriors of the villages in order to drive goblins back long enough for everyone to evacuate to a safe fishing village.

The goblins did not have boats, so as long as people could flee into the ocean, they would be all right. That's what Galatine and Shien had hoped, anyway.

In the end, however, they only successfully rescued two settlements. All other times, the pair had no choice but to retreat as they were now.

"No!"

Shien suddenly let out a cry of despair. Galatine stood staring in shock.

A village was burning before their eyes. The blaze consumed the innocents they had bled to save.

"Stooooooooooooop!!!!" Galatine roared, clenching his war hammer as he rushed in. Fighting now was suicide, yet Shien ran in alongside his friend. His Cleric blessing demanded he bring an end to the meaningless loss of life.

The two were surely charging into certain doom, and were quickly surrounded by goblins for their effort.

"Dammit!"

Galatine was barely an adult. Tears formed in the corners of his eyes as he glared at his hated enemies. There was no hope of victory anymore. Each goblin Galatine and Shien were up against rivaled the two in level.

Yet the pair did not falter, determined to bring down as many as they could with them.

"Arctic winds, life-stealing chill! Howl and roar! Blizzard!"

Powerful ice magic extinguished the flames and blew away the goblins.

Galatine and Shien stood dumbfounded, unsure what had happened and shocked to still be breathing.

As the frigid storm settled, they were finally able to see who had come to the rescue.

"Get 'em!" a woman shouted.

Twenty powerful, cutlass-wielding pirates charged the goblins who'd been staggered by the ice spell. A sailing ship had landed on the beach, and buccaneers with bows lined the deck, showering the monsters with arrows.

A beautiful woman led this band of outlaws. It only took a few moments before the goblins were running, and the young woman who was Galatine and Shien's savior approached them.

"Adventurers of this land! Your valorous struggle is clear from the wounds you bear!" She held out her hand to the two of them. "I've got experience fighting the goblin king's army! All I need is some military support and no goblin in the world will be a match for us!"

"What?!"

"Guide me to Zoltan! I'll take command! My name's Mistorm, and I'll exterminate every last one of those monsters! I swear by my ship, the *Regulus*!"

Mistorm flashed the sort of ferocious grin that was characteristic of pirates.

The young Galatine and Shien were bewildered and bewitched by the lovely woman's face.

Chapter 3

Assassins and the Assassins Guild

The young monk who had guided Red and friends into the back office of the holy church was walking on a side street during the evening. His steps were quick as he made his way toward the city gate from downtown.

"Heh."

A smile crossed his face. Bishop Shien had promised that the holy church would protect those families of devouts who lived outside of town.

The monk's family lived in a small farming settlement about a thirty minutes' walk toward the sea from Zoltan. He was on his way there now.

Their landlord was not a bad person, but with their harvest being split between the local lord, the landlord, and the holy church, the monk's family did not have anything left for themselves. They managed to get by on potatoes and beans they grew in the small plot behind their home. The monk was the second son of his family, and had been born with the Divine Blessing of the Cleric.

When it had been decided that he would join the Zoltan holy church, his kin celebrated with a delicious stew of potatoes and ground meat—something he had never had before—along with wheat biscuits and apple cider.

That night, his mother had apologetically given him warm-looking, patchwork long underwear.

"It doesn't look like much, but I was worried you'd catch a cold. Be sure to wear it at night."

The monk had treasured the piece of clothing and had never caught a chill, even on winter eves.

He dreamed of running a small holy church himself and supporting his family there so they could live an easier life. The goal was still very distant, but with the recent crisis, he was allowed to bring his family to the most splendid building in Zoltan, its cathedral.

Despite the emergency, the monk was glad that, for the first time, he could actually provide something for his family.

After kicking a pebble, the young devout snapped back to his senses and looked ahead.

A man was sitting in the middle of the road. There was a large ax placed on the ground in front of him, glinting with moonlight.

Getting a bad feeling, the priest decided to turn around and take another route. But two more men were already approaching from behind. Panicking, he tried to flee down a narrow alley between two fences.

"Argh!"

The monk found himself knocked to the ground. Yet another person had been lurking in the alley—a broad-shouldered, well-built man. The monk recognized his face.

"Y-you're from the Thieves Guild!"

Bishop Shien had protected a prostitute who had fled from her boss. This was that boss.

The monk knew nothing of the underworld, but he had heard Bishop Shien and one of the underlings of the fearsome Bighawk talking once.

"I think you owe me somethin'."

The man had a fearsome club studded with nails in one hand. He grinned down at the monk.

The young devout had only led the prostitute into the back of the holy church while Bishop Shien stood in her boss's way. He had certainly felt a swell of righteous indignation when he saw all the scars on her body, but he had not actually done anything to this man directly.

Obviously, the boss was uninterested in such technicalities and was looking to vent some frustration.

"Oy, don't kill him yet. We're using him to blackmail the bishop," one of the ruffians approaching from behind said.

His thief's blade was colored black to better blend into the night.

"Tch. I know, I know. Don't go orderin' me around."

"What's that? You talkin' back to me?"

"Don't go actin' all high an' mighty, mister *former* candidate for the big leagues! You're just a piece of shit like me now."

"The hell'd you say?!"

Bloodlust swelled from the man with the sword, but the one with the club displayed no sign of backing down, his rotted teeth showing as he scowled.

"If you wanna kill each other so bad, just say the word when we're done. I'll gladly end the both of you. Right now, you do what I say," commanded the man with the ax, silencing the arguing pair.

"I—I ain't gonna go against you." The ruffians all nodded in agreement with the one who spoke, fear on their faces.

The monk was terrified and couldn't stop trembling.

"Don't kill him, just break a leg. It'd be a pain if he ran," instructed the ax wielder. He stood and sauntered over. His weapon was large enough that it was difficult to imagine a human handling it.

"Eep!"

The monk tried to flee, but the man with the club tripped him, sending the poor devout tumbling to the ground again. "Heh-heh. Guess I'll let you off with just a leg then." He raised his weapon.

The monk wasn't accustomed to combat, and thus did the worst thing he could have: He closed his eyes, leaving himself defenseless.

"Ah?"

Before the brute with the club could strike, someone caught his hand from the dark.

* * *

"W-who're you?!"

I twisted his arm.

"Owww! Leggo!!"

The club thudded to the ground, and I knocked its owner aside.

"Gah! I'll fucking murder you!!!"

Enraged, he swung at me with his fist, but I dodged and landed a solid punch straight to his face.

"Ghck?!"

The man went flying and crashed to the ground. It didn't seem like he'd be getting up for a while yet. Blood ran from his nose.

"If you run that way, you'll be safe. Just keep moving and don't look back," I instructed.

"Y-yes, sir!"

The young monk scurried off as quickly as his legs could manage. Trading places with him, I stepped into the street.

"Y-you're that asshole Red!"

"Now, what could I have done that a thief remembers my name?" I said.

"Don't play dumb with me! Whose fault d'ya think it is that we're doing shit like this?!"

The brutes drew their swords.

An awkward, knowing smile formed on my face. "Ahhh. Now I understand."

The thieves froze with their weapons still drawn.

"I've been wondering who was lurking in the dark so stealthily."

The men collapsed to the ground like puppets whose strings had been cut. There was a small shadow behind them.

"That's my line, Red."

With a concerned expression, Tisse confirmed that the two she'd dispatched were unconscious.

When Rit, Ruti, and I had left after speaking to Bishop Shien, I'd noticed an unsavory group was watching the cathedral.

Recalling what Godwin had said, I had Rit and Ruti go home first and watched the situation from the shadows. When the men started tailing the monk, I had followed.

"I've been on guard because I noticed a presence so faint it felt like my imagination," Tisse stated.

"You took the words out of my mouth. I was on edge wondering what manner of powerful enemy capable of hiding so well was lurking in the alley," I replied.

That was why I had waited until the last moment before helping the monk. Tisse and I had both been hesitant because we were wary of each other.

I turned to the one remaining opponent, the man with the big ax. "So, that just leaves you. That's a pretty large weapon you've got there."

The blade of it was about as wide as an adult's torso.

"Taking your time chatting in front of me… Backwater adventurers really lack a sense of danger," the man spat with a sneer. "I'm Bloody Jack from the Assassins Guild."

"Did you say the Assassins Guild?"

What was this guy doing introducing himself?

I glanced over at Tisse. Her eyes were filled with disgust.

"This ax here's called the Giantslayer. A hero once felled a sun giant, one of the strongest kinds of giants, with this very weapon."

Why was he introducing his ax, too?

I glanced over at Tisse. She was looking down, as if in shame.

"Hey, Tisse, you think he's actually a member of the Assassins Guild?"

"That should go without saying. Please leave this to me."

"Hm? I don't mind, but..."

Compared to his Giantslayer, Tisse's shortsword was like a sewing needle. At a glance, it didn't look particularly reassuring. However, I could feel a tremendous murderous intent coming from Tisse, though the man she would fight hadn't noticed yet. Perhaps that was because Tisse had learned how to mask her feelings as a hired killer.

"What's that, little lady? You want to fight me by yourself?"

"Yes. You said that you are from the Assassins Guild, so that makes dealing with you my job."

"You got a score to settle with the guild? Heh-heh. Fine by me. I love killing people who're out for revenge."

Everything he said seemed to tick Tisse off. The more he spoke, the more her fury swelled.

If I was up against her in her present state, I'd run. Yet this guy didn't appear to notice his impending demise. He was all smiles as he pulled a vial from his cloak and downed its contents.

"Nrgh!"

His muscles swelled.

"Power of Gorilla! I have the strength of a great ape now!"

He grabbed his Giantslayer in both hands and swung it up over his head.

Ahhh, so he needs magic potions to lift his weapon, I thought.

"What do you think, girlie?! My Giantslayer ain't just for show!"

"It's unnecessary."

"What?!"

Tisse stepped forward, entirely unafraid.

"Dumbass! I'll split you in two!"

The man brought Giantslayer down, splitting the road with a loud crash. By the time it made impact, Tisse had already vanished, though.

"An assassin has no need for that clumsy weapon, nor such loose lips. In fact, I would be hard pressed to find any aspect of you that's appropriate for the job." She had already slipped close enough that she could strike with her blade. "An assassin needs only a weapon capable of piercing their target's heart. Nothing more."

The man dropped to his knees, still grinning. He'd probably never realized he was going to die.

* * *

"My apologies."

"There's nothing to apologize for. He was serious about killing you."

The young monk had run to Shien, so we left the cleanup of the incident to the local members of the holy church.

The three thieves had been hurt badly, but they would live. The self-proclaimed assassin was a different matter, though.

Tisse and I were sitting on a stair by the side of the road, eating some *oden*.

She had gone to get the food from the stall we frequented, and while the flavor was still good, it had gone cold and hard during the trip back here.

"When he brought the guild into it, it became my job to kill him," Tisse explained.

"Part of the Assassins Guild's code?"

"The guild rules are not as strict as most outsiders think. It's actually a similar system to the Adventurers Guild. It's a strictly offer-based system, which sets it apart, but it's up to each assassin to decide whether to take a job or not."

"So you don't have to kill someone if you don't want to?"

"Yes. And if you take a job, but decide you can't finish it, you can pass it off to another. We rescue any comrades who mess up and are captured, too. Members can retire when they please as well."

"Now that you mention it, I remember some assassins escaping prison back in the capital."

"There's no changing the role expected of the Assassin blessing, but at least we can live decent lives. Those in the guild are never to be treated as disposable. That's the entire reason the organization exists."

Mister Crawly Wawly was rubbing Tisse's shoulder gently. Her eyes narrowed a bit as she gently massaged the spider's stomach.

"The guild's formal stance on never carrying out a hit that disrupts society is just a pretext to protect itself from formal retaliation by nations."

"Really? The Assassins Guild is feared just about everywhere I've been. Even in Avalonia…," I said.

"A useful façade to hide behind," Tisse responded.

Her changes in expression were still quite minor, but I recognized the smile on her face. She looked like someone letting me in on a secret.

"The Assassin blessing thrives in situations where its users can operate at an advantage. If we were faced with an overwhelming army, we'd have no hope of winning. So then what do we do to keep from being wiped out? Thoughts like that are always on our minds."

Assassins went against the laws of society. But the Assassin blessing was Demis's will like every other, and some people wanted to live in accordance with the urges of that blessing. Ultimately, the impulses of a Divine Blessing were more powerful than mortal laws. Thus assassins created a guild in order to protect themselves.

That was what Tisse was saying.

The Assassins Guild was the largest organization of hired killers, and it wielded influence throughout the continent, but there were also similar, lesser groups.

In Avalonia, there had been the Band of the Scorpion, who had taken a job from the demon lord's army to take out Ruti. Unlike the guild, which only gathered people with blessings from the assassin line, this group picked up orphans and subjected them to harsh training, brainwashing them to become disposable pawns.

Those organizations existed for the purpose of covert killing, while the Assassins Guild existed to help assassins.

"The Assassins Guild is always at odds with those other hitman-type groups. It's a foundational difference in doctrine."

"Ahh."

"That's why the guild dictates that any assassin who misrepresents themself as a member of the guild must be killed. It hurts our reputation. And any strays who leave to take jobs the guild disapproves of cannot be tolerated."

"I've heard rumors about former members facing off against the guild," I commented.

"It's fine to leave if you aren't going to work as an assassin. The guild believes that each person is free to choose whether to kill or not. But taking reckless jobs is unacceptable," Tisse said.

"That makes sense."

The guild's goal was to create a place for assassins among society. Any who caused trouble threatened that object.

"Tisse... Did you come across something that's bothering you?" I was a little unsure whether I should say something. Still, she was my friend.

Tisse exhaled as Mister Crawly Wawly patted her shoulder.

"Mister Crawly Wawly... You're right. It's my problem to deal with, but..." Tisse paused and looked forward before continuing. "There are signs of real assassins in Zoltan—strays who left the guild."

"Real assassins?"

"I live as Ms. Ruti's friend now, but they're still my responsibility to handle."

"I don't know if they're who you mean, but I saw three people with Assassin blessings recently," I said.

Tisse's eyes went wide. "You did?! Could you please tell me more?"

"Well, I only got a glance..."

I told her what I knew about the people Rit and I had seen in the harbor district.

"There's no mistaking it. Those three are the strays," Tisse concluded. After listening to me, she seemed certain. All I had recounted were their blessing levels and general appearances, yet apparently, that was enough.

If she was that sure...

"Do you know them?"

Tisse's expression didn't change, but Mister Crawly Wawly cuddled up against her, as though to soothe the girl.

What a nice spider.

"I suppose the simplest way to put it is they were senior disciples ahead of me," Tisse replied. "We studied under the same master. We weren't close, but we lived together and shared meals."

"So they were comrades."

"Unlike with adventurers, it wasn't quite that level of bond. They were comrades in the sense that we shared an occupation, but that connection was gone once it became clear they were taking work from outside the guild's system."

"You've made it sound like the Assassins Guild offers a fairly reasonable environment. Why would anyone leave?" I questioned.

"Evidently, killing whomever they pleased suited their personalities better. The guild rejects quite a lot of requests."

Guild work was not steady, apparently. Those in charge tried to manage it so that members could get enough jobs to satisfy their impulses. However, blessings didn't just cause pain; they also brought joy. Assassins who longed to kill surely felt limited by the guild's methods.

"Anyway, I'll need to slay those three," stated Tisse.

I thought about that for a moment.

"...Would you like me to do it?"

"Eh?" Tisse's expression froze in shock. "I could never. You have your slow life. There's no reason for you to get involved."

"I can't imagine you want to kill people you know, right? It's not like I suddenly became a pacifist when I settled down here. I just don't join battles I don't want to fight."

"I appreciate your concern. You really are Ms. Ruti's brother. Still, I'll be fine. I call them senior disciples, but I don't really have any affection for them," Tisse responded with a shrug.

As best I could tell, that was how she genuinely felt. Tisse was an assassin. She wouldn't hesitate or show any mercy.

"They are targets to be dispatched." Tisse stood up, signaling the end of our discussion. "Shall we go back, then? We have people waiting for us."

"I guess so…," I replied. I quickly realized something, however. "Actually, no."

"What is it?"

"I feel like having some warm *oden*. Let's stop by Oparara's stand first."

Tisse nodded. "That sounds good."

We set off down the moonlit road together.

* * *

Three hours later, Tisse was on a road on the south side of downtown Zoltan, having split up with Red. She was holding a bag with a container of *oden* as she walked along the road.

Mister Crawly Wawly was hanging from her arm, peeking into the bag. Within was some food for Ruti: chicken balls, daikon, beef tendon, and an egg.

There was no *chikuwa* because the price of fish had gone up. *Chikuwa* was made from minced fish meat, and a small stall like Oparara's could not afford to keep stocking it now. Oparara tried to deal with it by selling things like chicken balls, but the taste wasn't the same.

"Hahhh. Curse those Veronian fiends…!"

For Tisse, who firmly believed that *chikuwa* was the pinnacle of *oden*, the Veronian galley had become an intolerable presence.

Her investigation over the past few days was reaching its final stage.

Difficult though it was to get news from beyond Zoltan's borders, there were still people to ask, from the Veronian sailors to all the other people who had brought in things to trade from foreign lands.

Tisse also had information from the Assassins Guild, though it was several months old now.

So the pirate king who conquered the seas of three different countries now lies on his death bed…

As the ruler of Veronia, King Geizeric couldn't let his weakness show, given the delicate state of the world. He attended important ceremonial functions and gave the utmost care to prevent domestic political issues. However, there was still no concealing that his time was almost up. Having faced death countless times as an assassin, Tisse understood from her intel that the man's end was near.

I suppose I should get started.

Tisse ducked into a rarely used alley, still carrying the bag of *oden* in her left hand as she drew her hidden sword.

"On to us, eh?"

A long-eared man emerged from the dark. It was one of the high elves on Prince Salius's ship.

While he was getting fired up at the prospect of a fight, Tisse looked annoyed and muttered to herself about having to battle twice in one day.

Unfortunately, the change in her expression was too slight to make those feelings apparent.

"You're no ordinary person, are you," the high elf remarked. He was holding a trident in his right hand and a folded-up net in his left.

Seems pretty clear he's got a Gladiator blessing, Tisse surmised.

Exceedingly few blessings specialized in such a unique combination of weapons. Gladiator favored fighting before a crowd. Naturally, the majority of its combat skills still worked without spectators.

The high elf grinned. "You're a strong one. But I'm not here to fight."

"Then what business do you have?" Tisse pressed.

"We've got your comrade. If you want her back safe, then come with me to the ship."

"..."

Tisse sunk into thought at that.

"Comrade" would presumably mean Ruti, but there's no one who could take her hostage. So Red or Rit, then? Yet even with a low estimation of their might, it'd take at least ten Veronian warships for a chance at capturing them... I can't really think of anyone they would have other than the stray cat Ruti and I are feeding. Does he mean those three assassins? No, that can't be...

Mister Crawly Wawly and Tisse were both at a loss.

"You seem surprised. I've got the Scouter skill, so I know when someone's blessing is a higher or lower level than mine. I'm level 39, and you surpass me. You can count the number of people in Veronia who outstrip me on one hand, so it's a shock to find a person like you in the middle of nowhere out here."

That's not too shabby, mused Tisse.

Were this high elf in the Assassins Guild, he'd be an elite, and in a band of knights, his strength would likely make him a company leader. His claim about being one of the best in Veronia was no empty boast.

That's not to say he was any match for Tisse, though.

"I also know just how weak that friend of yours in the armor was."

"?"

"There's no point hiding it. Her level was lower than mine. And my buddy who was with me has the Slave Hunter blessing. He's got a skill that works on enemies weaker than him, and we're the same level. Your friend's got no chance."

"???"

"Play dumb all you like. I know you're worried on the inside."

All I am is confused.

The situation was growing more befuddling by the minute.

Ruti's level was higher than Tisse's. There was no doubting she possessed the highest level in the world. How could that Slave Hunter's ability have registered it as lower?

Was it because he sensed New Truth?

Tisse, Rit, and Red all lacked a way to detect another's blessing. Red could guess fairly accurately, but that was only because of his research. Thus, they'd never known what would happen when someone with a skill that could analyze blessings tried it on Ruti.

So it picked up on New Truth instead of the Hero. I don't imagine someone with the Sage or Saint blessings who can use Appraisal will come to Zoltan, but Inquisitor and Witch Hunter can identify skills and blessing levels, too. If someone with one of those ran into Ruti and learned about New Truth, we could have a problem.

Mister Crawly Wawly leaped up at the gravity of the situation.

They would have to warn Ruti about this later.

"Oy, what are you doing getting lost in thought. Are you really higher level than me?" snapped the high elf. Tisse glowered indignantly, but because it did not show in her expression, the high elf continued to act superior. "I'll signal for my buddy to haul your friend over, so just be a good girl until then."

"I see…"

This guy doesn't realize how much danger he's in.

She owed him nothing, of course, but she suspected it was better to stop him from getting himself killed.

"You should really tell your partner to hurry over as quick as he can."

"Threatening me, eh? Beating me won't change a thing. Your friend is ours, and unless you do what you're told, she'll be subjected to some pretty gruesome torture. The Veronian navy's not kind. Even the strongest men end up bawling like babies, begging to die."

"No, that's not what I mean," Tisse stated, but it was no use.

"Plus, I've got the Divine Blessing of the Gladiator. I fight best one-on-one. From the way you dress, I'd guess you've got a blessing from the Thief tree. Can you really afford to act so calm?" The high elf smirked.

"She was probably getting ready for bed… Hopefully, she didn't kill him without asking questions first…," Tisse muttered pensively.

The high elf was getting more and more annoyed as the girl he'd hoped to intimidate continually ignored him.

"What, you one of those Demon-Possessed or Dual Mind types who can't be reasoned with?"

After a rude snort, the high elf pirate adopted a battle stance. He hadn't intended to fight, but if Tisse had a blessing that kept her from conversing normally, then he surmised it was equally probable she could attack at any moment. She might not even care about her friend being held captive.

The high elf flexed his arm holding the net, ready to move at a moment's notice.

"Bgh?!?!"

However, something came flying in from above with tremendous force, slamming into him before he had a chance to react.

"Huh?"

Even Tisse was shocked and required a moment to register what transpired.

There were now two high elves in front of her, and they both appeared in a pitiable state. Fortunately, their high levels had saved them from death.

"There's no way…" Tisse nervously turned around. The alley she was standing in was several hundred meters from Ruti's place.

She threw him?!

Everything Tisse knew of the world said that was beyond human capability. Ruti was no giant.

Wait, she actually tossed a giant one time.

Tisse remembered when the Hero's party had been attacked by a bunch of mountain giants. Ruti had not felt like dealing with them, so she stowed her sword, grabbed the mountain giants attacking her, and tossed them over a cliff in succession. It had ended with the giants running from Ruti in a twisted game of tag. That had happened shortly after Tisse had joined the group, making it a formative memory of sorts.

If Ruti could hoist such a massive creature, tossing a high elf must have been simple by comparison.

And she aimed for the other one, too.

Seeing the high elves twitching, Tisse let out a dry chuckle, her face still as expressionless as ever.

Ruti really is something.

* * *

The day after my evening with Tisse, I was dishing out plates full of pasta salad for breakfast as I listened to her explain what had happened after we'd split up.

"What did you do with them?" I asked.

"After Ms. Ruti healed the two, we tied them up and threw them in a room we weren't using."

"The *oden* was cold," Ruti remarked, picking a rather odd detail to get annoyed about. Her eyebrows flared slightly as she clenched her fists in front of her chest in an attempt to convey just how villainous the pair of pirates were.

Her definition of wickedness being that the *oden* had gone cold because of all the talking was probably why Tisse once claimed that Ruti's world was a bit askew compared to normal people's.

It was a quirk, to be sure. But I thought it was adorable!

"Hm." Tisse's lips spread into a bit of an odd expression, as if she had realized what I was thinking from the look on my face.

* * *

Come afternoon, Rit, Ruti, Tisse, Mister Crawly Wawly, Bishop Shien, and I met at the city gate.

Rit and I only had our shop to deal with, but Ruti, Tisse, and Bishop Shien had been running all around Zoltan. The ruffians from last night had been trying to blackmail Bishop Shien, who was the core of the faction opposed to giving in to Prince Salius. A higher-up in the Thieves Guild had apparently put them up to it. He had reached out to the remnants of Bighawk's faction to stir them to action.

Shien had demanded the Thieves Guild deal with the mastermind, but he also instructed the members of his clergy not to go out alone and to stay off the streets at night.

Obviously, it would have been nice if the city guards could help, but they were already short on staff. Maintaining the peace around town would probably fall to adventurers.

Moen was holding the high elves whom Lilinrala had sent in his jail. However, he was still holding back on reporting their capture to the Zoltan authorities. A decision would be made after seeing how Lilinrala's side reacted.

Unfortunately, there was also trouble brewing with the Merchants Guild, too. It was the organization hit the hardest by the present circumstances.

"You've been working hard."

"I have been. Pet me more." Ruti's eyes narrowed as she urged me to keep stroking her head.

During my time in the Hero's party, I had been the one in charge of diplomatic matters, yet Ruti had been handling those in Zoltan all on her own since yesterday.

I was happy to see her growing, but it was also a little sad. Perhaps that was the fate of all older siblings.

"I'm sad I can't go with you, but leave Zoltan to me."

Over the past few days, Ruti had become a big figure in town. Before this, the bigwigs in Zoltan had relied more on Tisse. The two girls were similarly stone-faced, but Tisse was easier to understand how to deal with than Ruti, who did things in such unorthodox ways. All that changed when the Veronian galley arrived, however.

Ruti had united the panicking people and conducted herself well, both in her actions and her instructions to others.

"I did it all just like you taught me, Big Brother," she whispered proudly.

I was certainly happy to hear that. The Hero's journey had been filled with difficulty for Ruti, but it was good to know our time together hadn't been for nothing.

My little sister had absorbed all the knowledge I'd learned as a knight and meshed it with her own abilities. My little sister was perfect… Other than her communication skills, of course… Everyone had their weak points, though.

Her deeds had earned her the trust of Zoltan's leaders, to the point that they'd listen to her instructions without protest. Ruti had it all under control, making her capable of accomplishing more in Zoltan at the moment than even Galatine or Moen. That's why she had to stay behind instead of coming with us into the forest.

"I'm sorry you ended up with all the responsibility, Ms. Ruti," Tisse apologized.

Ruti smiled and shook her head. "You are closer to Mistorm than I am. If one of us needs to stay behind, then it should be me."

"Ms. Ruti…"

Perhaps my sister's social skills were better than I thought.

Tisse's friendship was gradually pushing Ruti to change for the better. And that filled me with joy.

"All right, shall we head out?" Bishop Shien proposed after checking the condition of the riding drakes.

The four creatures belonged to the holy church, and had an excellent shine to their brown scales. They had been well cared for.

"Gyah."

One of the drakes bumped my head with a horn.

It seemed a little uneasy. Maybe it was a bit finicky?

I massaged around its chin to relax it as I stepped into the stirrup and swung myself onto the saddle.

"Gyahhh!" the drake roared happily. Its unease seemed to give way to the excited anticipation of being able to run to its heart's content.

* * *

It was cloudy today.

The colorful grasslands had dulled in color from the cold winter.

"Grrrrr..."

"Don't get down."

The drakes were walking leisurely instead of running.

Mine seemed upset at not being able to stride quickly across the wide-open plain, its body trembling and nostrils flaring in protest.

I patted the base of the drake's horns to soothe it.

"Gahh."

It looked like that managed to help a bit.

"Mistorm and Yarandrala are staying in a settlement hidden from the people of Zoltan. I'd rather not rush in and draw attention," Shien explained as he chuckled awkwardly at our irritated mounts.

"Even so, it can't be too far, right?" I asked.

"Yes, we should arrive in about an hour at this rate."

It was nice to have the riding drakes, since we were passing over wild land with no roads. The beasts didn't falter once, even on softer terrain.

"Are there any signs of someone following us?" I asked.

Hearing that, Rit's ears—wolf ones—perked up and twitched. She sniffed a few times and then nodded.

"Yeah, it's fine! There's no one nearby."

She was using a spell called Aspect of Wolf. As the name implied, it enabled the user to adopt a wolf's senses.

Aspect spells belonged in the category of transformation ones. By using them, you gained some physical qualities of a particular beast.

There were four categories of transformation magic: power, aspect, form, and shape.

Power spells granted a portion of the creature's ability, but the user remained physically unaltered. So with Power of Wolf, you would add a wolf's muscular strength to your own.

However, the aspect, form, and shape spells all changed your body. Form of Wolf shifted the caster into a bipedal lupine being. Shape of Wolf allowed you to become a wolf proper. As for Aspect of Wolf…

"Hmhm♪"

There was a bushy wolf tail poking out from under Rit's skirt, swaying back and forth as we rode through the field. Furry ears were poking from her head, too.

That was how aspect spells operated. They granted you a few visible qualities of the animal.

It was so…cute. I found myself really wanting to pet Rit's head.

"?"

Seemingly noticing my gaze, Rit turned around.

That's a wolf's senses for you. I waved my hand to say it was nothing and looked away, a little embarrassed.

"Hey, Red."

"Hm? What is it?"

Rit slowed her drake a bit to ride beside me. "Hup!" She stood up in the saddle and batted her tail against my cheek.

"So fluffy."

"Right?" Rit laughed, her wolf ears flitting. "I was surprised, too. It's my first time using a wolf spell. I've done Aspect of Otter, Bat, and I tried Elk once before, too."

I would love to see a round-eared otter Rit with a long, thin tail and an impish-looking bat Rit.

"...An elk?" I questioned.

"They do well in the cold and don't get tired trekking over snowy mountains. It's a good fit for Loggervia's climate," Rit answered.

I was imagining Rit covered with soft fur, but the spell shouldn't have been capable of something that significant.

"When I used Aspect of Elk, umm, my legs got really, really muscular, so... I'd rather not show that one off."

Aww.

Aspect magic was certainly intriguing. When things calmed down, perhaps we could try a few.

* * *

A forest grew in the middle of some marshy wetland approximately thirty kilometers from Zoltan.

Countless thin trees with twisted roots extended from the mud. It was an uncommonly dark place for Zoltan.

"Hardly seems like a pleasant spot to live," I commented when I saw my drake sink all the way to its knees in the soft earth.

"I agree," Bishop Shien responded. He sounded almost sad.

The hidden settlement where Mistorm and Yarandrala were hiding lay somewhere in these woods. Since it was a village, that suggested others resided there, too.

"Woah there."

I sliced a lesser slime that suddenly dropped from a tree.

Lesser slimes possessed no intelligence, so it hadn't been aiming for me. Rather, it had just conveniently dropped when a target was below. That's what I thought, anyhow.

Rit's wolf ears twitched. "There's something up there," she said.

A moment later, a shower of lesser slimes fell from above.

Shien wasted no time intoning a spell. "Wind of righteous destruction and revelation! Tornado Cutter!"

A furious wind swirled above our heads. The raging gale shredded the monsters, destroying them all.

"Not good! Not good!"

I caught a hushed voice from above. Monsters that looked like humanoid frogs were fleeing, hopping from branch to branch. These creatures were called grippas.

They were skilled at climbing trees using the sticky fluid they produced from their hands, and they were relatively intelligent. Grippas were even known to use weapons made by humans that they found.

Evidently, they were the ones that had dropped the slimes on us. I guess they'd hoped to catch us off guard while we were dealing with the barrage.

"Should we chase after them?" I inquired.

"No, our goal isn't to slay monsters," Bishop Shien responded. "Also, the grippas help keep others away from this place," he added with a mysterious sort of grin. "As a member of the clergy, I can't condone monsters that threaten human safety, but..."

"I get it. Sorry for asking."

The people of this secluded village wanted their home to remain that way.

Zoltan was the gathering ground of people who had fled from other lands. There was a tacit understanding not to pry. This place wasn't too different, in a way.

After another five minutes of slogging through the marsh, we arrived at the secret village.

* * *

A single old man was sitting on a tree root.

"What's this… You folks get lost and stumble all the way here?"

He looked like hunter. He wore a bearskin, had a staff in his hands, a bow at his side, and a knife carved out of a deer's antler at his waist. There was no trace of metal anywhere on him.

"Gomes. You look to be doing well. It's me, Shien."

"Oh, Shien. Nice of you to stop by."

The old man's wrinkled face broke into a smile. He could hardly open his eyes because of how thick his lids had become, but what little of them was visible was a cloudy white. He must have had some very serious cataracts. Normally, it would be impossible to use a bow like that.

"You seem a little haggard, Shien. Have you been eating enough?"

"Hah-hah, I've been so busy lately that self-care has fallen by the wayside."

"That's no good. You have to make time to eat. Anything can be managed on a full stomach. Oh, did you get a new riding drake?"

"Heh, I've been entrusting caring for the riding drakes to others, regrettably."

"You should know better."

"Red, he's…" Rit began.

"Yeah, he's got the Wind Druid blessing."

What's more, he had to be near level 30, high enough to rival a knight from the capital. Although blind, Gomes must have been able to sense things via the whispers of the spirits.

"It's rare for you to bring visitors."

"Yarandrala's friends," Shien replied. "They came because they are worried about her."

"Well now, hmm, I can see an odd color about you. You're something."

"My name is Red. This is my partner, Rit, and my friend, Tisse."

"And a small spider as well," Gomes added.

Tisse smiled slightly at that. Mister Crawly Wawly popped his head out of her bag and waved his right leg in greeting.

"His name is Mister Crawly Wawly."

"A Mr.... Crawly Wawly?"

"The Mister is part of his name."

"That's a pretty unique moniker, but it has a nice ring to it. Yeah, that's a good name." Gomes grinned as he stood. "Well then, let me show you to the village."

"Thank you."

The blind hunter moved slowly at first, relying on his staff.

We dismounted from our drakes to follow, and our boots immediately sank into the mud.

* * *

There was a gathering of small buildings in the gaps between trees.

Unlike the zoog village from our previous trip, a simple human settlement like this generally used earthen walls and tree trunks to make little huts.

"Hey Shien, long time no see."

"Guests? When you're done, tell us a bit about the outside world."

"Have you had lunch yet?"

People called out to Bishop Shien in greeting, and they showed an interest in us, too.

"They're all quite elderly," Tisse remarked quietly.

A few homes looked to have been vacant for a while, suggesting that no one new was moving here.

"Not only that, they are all pretty high-level," I responded.

"Really?" Tisse asked.

Nodding, I explained, "Generally in the low to mid 20s, I think, putting them on the lower side of B-rank adventurers. Age has probably dulled their strength a bit, but… A group like this in Zoltan would have made things very different."

And yet, they'd chosen to remain here.

In Zoltan, they could have become heroes like Albert, yet they'd elected to hide from the world.

There was a slightly larger structure that stood out from all the others in the village. The other homes were made of wood from trees in the marsh, but this one had been constructed from more solid lumber.

The ground had been paved with magically adhered sand and rock. It showed no signs of shifting, despite the unevenness of the swamp.

"Young Miss!" Gomes called out.

Young Miss?

"Okay, okay! Sheesh! What do you think you're doing, calling me that in front of my youthful friends!"

The door opened, and Mistorm stepped out, and beside her…

"Why did you follow me?"

Yarandrala looked a bit troubled, though there was a pleased smile on her face.

* * *

"So, care to explain yourself?" I said.

"I could ask the same of you."

Yarandrala puffed out her cheeks and looked to one side. "You've

already stepped away from the front lines. You should leave things to your reliable big sister."

"Big sister, huh?"

It had been a while since I heard that.

Yarandrala had become my friend shortly after I'd arrived in the capital, when I was still just a boy. Whenever I attempted to help her with a dangerous problem, she always tried to brush me aside with that line. Hearing it was pretty nostalgic.

We first met when I was in the Bahamut Knights, back when I was nine. I was a kid alone in the big city, and Yarandrala was one of the few people I could speak freely with.

At the time, she really had been something like a much older sister. Honestly, the title was pretty fitting. Unfortunately, Yarandrala was only half reliable. The other half was always sticking her nose into trouble the moment you stopped watching her.

"It feels like you're thinking something really disrespectful," Yarandrala said, narrowing her eyes at me. "Hahhh… Whatever. I get it. I should have at least let you know."

"Obviously. If it was something you could handle alone, I would have still happily supported you. And were it anything larger, I'd pitch in directly. You would have been really upset if I'd done this to you."

"W-well, yeah, I guess so. But is this all right with you, Rit?" Yarandrala inquired.

"Me?" Rit looked a bit surprised when the conversation suddenly shifted to her, but she quickly fired back, "I'm upset."

Her face was honestly a little scary. Yarandrala was her dear friend as well as mine. It was no surprise to hear she was angry that the high elf had up and vanished.

"I'm sorry." Yarandrala finally acknowledged her mistake.

"Now now, don't give the poor girl too much of a hard time. I'm the one they're seeking, so it's my fault."

Mistorm had gone to get some tea and returned just in time to defend Yarandrala.

"That being the case, could you please explain the situation?" Tisse asked once Mistorm sat down.

*   *   *

"An opponent who pushed you to your limit and managed to escape from Yarandrala while carrying his wounded friends...," I muttered.

Apparently, Yarandrala had been looking for Mistorm on the night of the festival for two reasons.

The first was because Mistorm had cast Demon's Flare, a spell used by upper-tier demons in the demon lord's army. It was a fearsome spell that transformed magic power into flames and then loosed them in a terrible blaze. A single mage could change the course of a fight with Demon's Flare. It was enough to push back an army of thousands. When the demon lord's army unleashed it in battle, our forces had been wiped out. Even the Bahamut Knights had been grievously injured. It had pushed us to the brink of a total collapse.

How was Mistorm able to use a spell that powerful? Had I seen her cast it back when I was a member of the Hero's party, I would have investigated. I'd elected not to, though.

However, Yarandrala was different. She hadn't given up the life of a hero to take it easy. Mistorm had caught her interest, and she had investigated.

Because she was on her guard, Yarandrala had noticed the stray assassins pursuing Mistorm sooner than anyone else. No matter how skilled the hired killers were, they weren't going to slip past a Singer of the Trees who could communicate with plants. Not unless they knew she was watching for them beforehand.

And that was the second reason. While Yarandrala had been enjoying the festival with us that day, she had also been in contact with the flora, keeping an eye on Mistorm, and she'd rushed to the older woman's side the moment she detected danger.

"He was stronger than I expected, though," Yarandrala admitted with a frown. "I thought Mistorm would be able to fend off most anyone, so I panicked a little when she got concerned. I also hadn't expected him to be able to escape my magic."

"Prince Salius's battleship hadn't arrived at that point. If you'd known this was more than some local Zoltan issue, then you might have guessed someone with a high blessing level was involved… You could have come to me about this, you know," I said.

"Mgh." Yarandrala looked a little pained.

"I would have noticed his level, and if the two of us fought together, there's no way he would have escaped."

"That's…"

"You can't protect Mistorm and go after those responsible. That's why you've been staying here, locked in a stalemate, right? I'm sure it's been frustrating."

"…Yeah. I was actually struggling with what to do next."

Even if Yarandrala was a great hero who had battled it out with the demon lord's army countless times, she was still only one person.

"Next time, please let me know what's going on. I promise I won't butt into things you can take care of yourself. I'm glad you care so much about our quiet life, but I don't want you getting hurt over it."

"That's pretty selfish," chided Yarandrala.

"That's the whole point—living our lives the way we want."

We smiled at each other.

"Red."

Rit suddenly wrapped her arm around me from behind.

"Y-yes?" I replied.

"What was that about 'if the two of us fought'?"

"Hn? Ah..."

"After you said all that, did you plan on excluding me?"

Rit's grip on me tightened.

It was lovely to feel her warmth, but it was right on the line where if she put any more strength into her squeezing, it would really hurt.

"I'm sorry. It was a slip of the tongue," I assured her.

"Very well, then."

It truly had been an honest mistake. Mistorm grinned at us.

"You make a good party," she commented.

"Hah-hah, I must be getting old. It's almost too much for me," Shien added.

Undoubtedly, they were recalling their own youthful days as adventurers.

A good party...

I had been pushed out of mine and suffered for it. Things were better now, however. Maybe we really did make a good party. Without realizing it, I had broken into a pleasant smile. The tranquil mood in the room ended abruptly, though, as a shout from outside rang out.

"What's that? I'll go take a look real quick."

Bishop Shien stood and headed for the door.

"I'll come with you," I said.

"If you're going, then I'm coming, too," Rit declared, and we both followed Shien.

"You take care of things here, Yarandrala, Tisse," I instructed.

The little assassin nodded. "Understood."

An ominous feeling settled into my gut. I rested my hand on the hilt of my sword.

* * *

Stepping outside, we saw two riding drakes running wild.

The old villagers were trying to calm them, but the beasts showed no signs of stopping.

"What's going on?"

The riding drakes were the property of the holy church. They should have been carefully trained, so Bishop Shien rushed toward them when he saw them behaving oddly.

"Wait, Bishop! Get away!" I shouted.

I sensed a wicked intelligence and malice in the riding drakes' red eyes.

"Those aren't our drakes!"

The creatures leaped into the air and slashed at Shien with their talons. Yet though Shien had grown old, he was still a hero like Mistorm, and had safeguarded Zoltan for decades. He protected his vitals with his left arm and quickly formed a seal with his right hand.

"Tch. What are you? Tornado Cutter!"

A swirl of magic wind swallowed up the two malicious riding drakes. It was no small feat to maintain focus and cast a spell while your arm was being cut.

Such a level of proficiency befit a champion of Zoltan. Unfortunately...

"What?!" Shien shouted.

The drakes transformed into half-drake, half-human forms and tore through the Shien's spell, closing in on him. The magic hadn't worked!

Both of our opponents were more powerful than the bishop.

"Not on my watch!"

"Tch?!"

Rit hurled a pair of throwing knives, shouting to draw the monstrous creatures' attention instead of hitting them while they were unaware. They both easily deflected the knives with their claws, but that gave Bishop Shien all the time he needed to move away.

"Hahhh!"

I used Lightning Speed to race forward, catching the drake hybrids off guard and tracing my blade across their stomachs.

The scales covering their bodies made them resilient enough that my bronze sword didn't manage to cut through to their skin. The two drake hybrids leaped backward, and their forms twisted, transforming into humans.

The clothes and swords that had melded into their altered bodies reappeared. I recognized them as two of the stray assassins from the harbor district.

"You really got us. To think you would use Shape of Riding Drake to hide. I shouldn't have missed that," I remarked.

"It's nothing to be ashamed of. We've trained to quiet our minds and allow the bestial instincts to control our bodies. It's impossible to see through without a Sage's Appraisal skill."

This pair had studied under the same master as Tisse, but their style was clearly very different. Tisse was the archetypical assassin, relying on stealth and blades. However, these two employed skills from the Assassin blessing that were closer to those found in the Mage tree.

They drew their shortswords and took a stance that resembled Tisse's. When it came to the fundamentals of combat, they truly had learned together.

Did that mean I could anticipate their moves?

I slowly lowered my sword, taking a lower stance as I kept my guard up.

"You're a strong one," one of the men said with a grin. "I like killing strong guys."

"How nice for you," I replied.

Bishop Shien was behind me.

His left arm was bleeding, but that had done little to weaken his fighting spirit. Still, for someone who had been out of the action for so long, it was a dangerous wound. He really needed to close it with magic as soon as possible, but he didn't know me well enough to entrust me with defense while he focused on recovery.

"Red, please focus on guarding. I'll provide support magic…!"

Shien was prioritizing aiding me—a standard decision.

It would take about twelve seconds for Rit to reach us. Until then, I would have to protect Bishop Shien and the people of the village alone. It was only twelve seconds, but that was more than enough time for the assassins to run someone through with a sword.

I focused on my opponents' movements while looking for an opening.

"You can have him, so let me kill the girl back there."

"First come, first serve."

"I know, I know. But her ass and legs felt crazy nice. I really wanna kill her."

What? Oh, so you were the drake Rit was riding. I see, I see… So you liked how her butt and thighs felt?

That didn't sit right with me. A switch flipped in my peace-dulled mind, and I instantly changed gears.

You think I care whether Bishop Shien sees?

I raised my sword, taking a more offensive stance.

"Mgh…"

Sensing the change, the stray assassins readied themselves. Unfortunately for them, they hadn't done so quickly enough.

Clang!

A cry of metal on metal sounded. The assassin was shocked that I'd closed the distance in a single step, but he managed to defend himself with his sword.

"Gah?!" he groaned in displeased surprise.

The moment our blades met, I pulled mine back and took another step past his and slashed again. My sword passed his defenses and cut into his shoulder deep enough to reach the bone. Even for a trained killer, it was enough to make him collapse.

"Tch!" The other stray assassin kept his calm as his comrade fell. He loosed a quick slash while my back was turned to him. I yanked my blade from the other man's shoulder as I spun and struck the attacker's fist. I could feel bone shattering. He faltered for only a brief moment, but that was enough for me to get in another strike.

"Gh…!"

With that, both assassins had been felled.

I slowly exhaled. Once I got heated up, it took some work to calm back down.

"I heard that you were strong, but to think you were this skilled…"

Bishop Shien was standing there in shock, having forgotten entirely to use any magic.

Uh oh, I really overdid things.

"Red!" Rit dashed over. "Is everything okay?!"

"Yeah, I'm fine."

"Phew! After I saw you turn so serious, I worried they might actually be pretty strong."

I smiled to help ease Rit's concern.

"We should return to Mistorm. That was only two of the stray assassins. There's still one more."

As if in reply, a large explosion went off. Fire erupted from the window of the house where Mistorm and the others were waiting. The blaze quickly spread over the building, but a giant tree rose from the ground inside the building without any concern for the flames around it.

"That's Yarandrala's Elder Treant!"

The massive wooden creature reached a hand out toward the blaze consuming the house. The fire gathered into a single mass and separated from the house. Within that mass of flames was the final stray assassin.

"I won't let you get away this time!" Yarandrala shouted from atop the treant's shoulder.

She looked utterly sure of herself because they were fighting in her natural element—the forest.

Mistorm leaped from the house a moment later. She had likely protected herself with a spell, because there wasn't even a speck of ash on her clothes.

"I've got my magic power fully recovered this time! Don't think this will be as simple as before!" Mistorm turned her staff on the assassin.

But instead of turning to face them, the hired killer looked in my direction.

"So you got both of them, huh?" he commented as he gazed at his fallen comrades. There was no trace of panic in his voice.

"And you'll meet the same fate soon!" Yarandrala cried.

The treant's arm stretched out to catch the man. Yarandrala wasn't using her signature spell, Thorn Bind, for fear of the fire magic. Fortunately, the assassin's flames couldn't burn down an Elder Treant.

"Hyahhhhh!" howled the assassin, swinging both of his arms wide. A storm of throwing knives buffeted the great tree creature, yet it weathered the onslaught without so much as slowing down.

"Did you really think that would work?" Yarandrala shouted.

"Martial art: Chain Explosion!"

The knives stuck in the Elder Treant's wooden body exploded in succession.

"Kh?!"

Yarandrala's massive summoned warrior trembled, rocked by the blasts, and she herself was knocked to the ground. Thankfully, the treant was fine. It had taken damage, but not enough that it couldn't continue.

The stray assassin had seized that opportunity to vanish, however.

"Dammit!"

He'd used a powerful martial art, but it hadn't been intended to take Yarandrala down. The man hadn't even bothered waiting to see if it had been effective or not.

"But this time, it looks like he didn't have the luxury to retrieve his friends," I said. Behind me, the two I had defeated were still lying on the ground.

If only the third assassin had come for his allies, we would have been able to stop him. Regardless, he was gone without a trace now. Were Ruti here, we'd be able to catch him, but pursuing as we were would be difficult.

"Wait, where's Tisse?" Rit asked.

I suddenly realized I hadn't seen her anywhere during the skirmish, either.

"Did she chase after him by herself?!" Rit hurriedly started to try to chase after them, but I stopped her.

"We can't follow them," I said.

"But!"

"Tisse didn't leave any tracks we could follow. That means she's sure that she can handle it alone."

She was planning to settle things alone.

* * *

The last stray assassin—Drog—had transformed into a half-human, half-drake hybrid using Form of Riding Drake and was running through the forest at high speed.

That he could do that without leaving any footprints spoke to the strength of his Assassin blessing. If a mage had tried this tactic, it wouldn't have worked.

It was only because the marsh had such muddy ground that made for poor footing that I was able to pursue. I would have to make sure to finish him here.

My name is Tisse Garland. I'm Ruti's friend and an assassin with the Assassins Guild. I'm currently running along the tree branches, chasing one of my own who betrayed the guild.

"Tch."

Drog's speed dropped slightly when he stepped on a rotten tree root.

I immediately threw a knife and twisted his body to dodge. Unsurprisingly, he'd been aware I was after him. Still, he'd had to slow down dramatically to recover after such an awkward motion.

"Tisse?!" Drog shouted when he saw me already in range to fight. "To think we would meet again like this! Did you take a job from the guild to get us?"

"I'm under no obligation to answer you."

I had not been given any such request. No one could have guessed that three top-class assassins-turned-traitors would end up in Zoltan. I'm sure he'd assumed people were onto him to be on the safe side, though.

And as expected, Drog appeared to be under the impression that if he didn't kill me, more from the guild would come.

We ran through the woods, drawing our swords at the same time.

"The two of us fighting… You were always a genius Tisse, but you only killed when the guild ordered it of you. I'll show you how murdering as I please has set me apart."

"I see. I take it you've gotten a lot of experience chatting, then?"

"You were always stuck up just because the master praised you, but everyone knew I was best in a real fight!"

Drog leaped into the air, his face warped in a savage scowl as he flew toward me.

I jumped at the same time as he did.

"An assassin's blade should bring fear like a star falling to earth."

"Still faithful to the master's teachings, even after leaving the guild."

We both kicked against trees, each aiming to get the high ground.

"“Ngh!”"

Neither of us shouted. There were only muffled grunts as we crossed paths in midair. No blade tasted blood.

"Not bad, but I know your moves now… You won't get another chance." Drog grinned as he landed on the ground.

I said nothing, readying my sword.

"Give it up. I'm clearly still on top. Why not join me, Tisse? I won't have to kill you, then."

What?

The offer wasn't nearly enough to make me question myself, but it was a surprise all the same.

"It's boring to live your life bound to the guild. Come with me and kill as you please. To reign over that which transcends things like good and evil is what it really means to be an assassin. All the wealth and power in the world mean nothing before a silent blade. In the moment an assassin kills, they become a god."

His words were disgusting.

"Drog..."

"Ready to give up?"

"Running your mouth before a kill is the sign of a third-rate assassin."

"So that's your answer... What a shame!"

Drog leaped again, certain he would win.

"W-what?!"

Instead of jumping to match him, I ran across the ground.

Drog appeared to be caught unaware at that, but he still struck. His attack used a style of swordsmanship built around pouncing from an advantageous higher position. It was the best way to take advantage of the specialization provided by the Assassin blessing. Our teacher had told us it was the textbook setup for an assassin's style.

Drog had misjudged our master's teachings, though. He and I were biased toward jumping and tended to go higher than necessary.

As a result, Drog believed he understood my skill level, but I had merely chosen to use a technique he knew, allowing him to see through it.

Catching the target in a moment when their guard was down was the key to a swift kill. Pouncing from the air was only one method for achieving that condition.

And my slash would be lethal. He would not have the time to use any tricks.

Our second exchange was very different from the first.

"Gah… Hah…"

Drog crashed into the ground, unable to land correctly. He tried to push himself up, but he could not gather the strength in his arms.

"You should be able to tell that's a lethal wound."

My blade had passed through the gap between his ribs and reached his internal organs. As Drog lay there bleeding and groaning, I approached to deliver the finishing blow.

"W-wait," Drog looked up at me. "Don't kill me."

Despite his actions, I couldn't hold it against him that he was begging for his life. The thought of dying was scary, even to a hired killer. There was no way I could allow a stray assassin who tarnished the guild's name to escape, however.

"I'll tell you who hired us… So please, just let me live."

Any empathy I felt for Drog before vanished after he said that.

Not revealing your client was the bare minimum standard for an assassin.

Drog had left the guild in order to slay indiscriminately; he had long since ceased being an assassin. Now he was only a common murderer.

"…Who hired you?"

I stifled my rage.

Whatever my personal feelings, this was crucial information for everyone else.

I had a faint hope that this was just Drog bluffing to catch me off guard. But unfortunately, I was wrong.

"It's the Veronian admiral, Lilinrala… She wanted us to kill Misphia, the first queen of Veronia… She's hiding in Zoltan under the name Mistorm."

"So it was Admiral Lilinrala."

Apparently, Mistorm's true name was Misphia—Queen Misphia, even.

I didn't know the details, but that would make her the first wife of King Geizeric, who went missing decades ago. So that galley, Drog, and Mistorm were all connected.

"I see. Thank you for that information."

"S-so then!"

"Yes, I won't finish you off."

I sighed as I turned away.

Even though I gave Drog a good opening, he made no attempt to pick up his sword. Instead, he grasped after a cure potion and drank it, glad to be alive.

I heard him coughing and vomiting up the potion.

"I won't finish you off, but that wound will kill you anyway. A potion won't save you now."

"Agh… Wait… I can't… see…"

"You should know the symptoms of blood loss. You've witnessed it plenty of times already, haven't you?"

I started walking away, not looking back.

Drog had been faithful to the impulses of his Assassin blessing, going so far as to leave the guild for them. The result was a far cry from the ideal assassin, however.

It was a mystery.

* * *

"Tisse's back!" Rit called out in relief.

The girl approached calmly with Mister Crawly Wawly on her shoulder.

Evidently, she had managed to take out her opponent.

"I'm back."

"Nice work."

I passed her a towel and some water that I had ready for her.

"Thank you."

High-level though Tisse was, chasing after someone fleeing through the forest and fighting them still took its toll. She slowly sipped the water and then wiped away her sweat.

"What did you do with the two you defeated, Red?"

"They're tied up in the shed," I replied.

"I see…"

"I'll explain things to everyone else, so you decide what to do with them."

"Thank you."

Tisse touched the hilt of the sword, and then stopped to look up at me as though searching for confirmation. I nodded. She began toward the shed but abruptly stopped.

"…I'm sorry, I shouldn't have done that," Tisse said.

"Hm?"

"If I check with you, I'm making you take responsibility for my job."

I was about to brush it off as nothing big, but Tisse's expression was more serious than I'd expected.

"Want me to come with you to the shed?"

I had everyone else head back inside before we went to deal with the two assassins.

"You know I used to be a soldier, and I've killed plenty of people, too. You don't need to go worrying about me," I commented.

"I know…"

Tisse was troubled because she had checked with me whether to kill the two assailants, and that meant that I had functionally decided to take their lives. She seemed disgusted with herself for that.

"I don't regret the killing itself. This is the blessing I was born with, and this is the life I've lived. But I also wish to have a reason for the act," Tisse explained.

"An assassin's job means killing people at someone else's request, so that's natural," I replied.

"I want more than that."

The shed wasn't far away by any means, and we were soon at the door.

"The stray assassins," Tisse whispered. "They were faithful to the impulses of their blessings. Almost certainly far more so than I am to mine. And yet, as assassins, they were impure and incomplete. Why?"

"That's simple," I responded.

Tisse looked up at me, a little surprised at how readily I answered.

"How so...?"

"All they did was obey their urges. But you think for yourself about the best course of action. That's really all there is to it."

"Maybe. Yet while I don't submit to my blessing, I'm still an assassin through and through."

"Hm?"

"...You and Ms. Ruti quit and chose to live a slow life. You stopped being a knight, and she gave up being the Hero. I haven't renounced my life as an assassin, but I'm still out here with you both."

"Ah."

"There are times when I wonder whether it is really okay for me to remain in Zoltan." Tisse looked down.

"Why wouldn't it be?" I asked lightly. "Ruti enjoys your company, and you feel the same way about her, right?"

"Yes, Ms. Ruti is someone I can look up to, and also—"

"She's like a troublesome little sister, yeah?"

"Hah-hah. Yes. It's a bit rude, but that's how I feel. She's extraordinarily strong and wise, and yet if you just leave her alone, she gets into trouble... It's a joy to be with her."

"There aren't many people who recognize her charms. Thank you, Tisse."

"Eh? There's no gratitude necessary. I stay with her because I want to."

Tisse's face reddened slightly in embarrassment. I smiled at the sight.

"Seems like there's no problem, then. Assassin or not, that doesn't change the fact that it's fun to be around your friends."

"Are you sure it's all right?"

"You don't have to deny that aspect of yourself for our sake. You can remain with Ruti while still being Tisse the assassin. The important part is just that you are Ruti's friend."

"Hmmm."

"I don't think anyone's interests line up perfectly. But so what? Ruti and I are your friends because we want to be."

"That's…true. I guess it's been so long since I've done proper assassin work that it got me wondering. Thank you."

"Look, this is just my opinion, but…" I paused, looking at Tisse, "I don't think your way of life is wrong. Can't you just stay how you are, an assassin living a slow life?"

"That's certainly an odd way to put it." Tisse smiled, and then her expression changed. "Okay, I've got a job to finish."

"Sure. I'll be waiting for you."

There were no sounds, but two of the presences in the shed were quickly snuffed out.

* * *

Tisse and I returned to Mistorm's house. The interior was blackened from the fire.

"I'm sorry for not noticing those three until it was too late," Tisse apologized.

"It's fine. Both Shien and my house will recover."

Bishop Shien had mended his wound with magic, but given his age, he had to lie down in bed to rest from the blood loss.

"If it's anyone's fault, it's his for not noticing that his own riding drakes had been switched out. He looks like he's got his head about him, but he's always been prone to messing up in the clutch," Mistorm remarked. Then she launched into a few old stories about Bishop Shien's previous blunders, which brought a pleasant smile to our faces.

"Whoops, the water should be ready now. I'll get some tea and treats," Mistorm said.

"Ah, let me help."

Tisse started to get up, but Mistorm gently waved her off.

"It's fine, it's fine. You're a guest, so just take it easy." The old woman headed off into the kitchen. After a couple of minutes, she returned holding a tray in her hands. "Help yourselves."

She set a bottle of rum and some cups on the table. Tisse, who didn't drink, looked curious and a bit surprised.

"It's a joke, dear."

There was a mischievous smirk on Mistorm's face as she gave everyone a cup of black tea. Then she mixed just the slightest bit of rum into each and dropped in little pieces of butter that floated on the surface of the dark liquid.

"Hot buttered rum?" I inquired.

"Yes. You know your stuff."

It was a warm drink suited for cold days. A guy who grew up in the South had told me about it during my tenure with the Bahamut Knights.

"In Veronia, sailors would bring home leftover rum, and their mothers or wives would use it for cooking or cocktails. The taste of rum became synonymous with family harmony."

"So you really are from Veronia," Tisse commented.

"I am indeed."

Tisse drank a sip of the hot buttered rum and then exhaled.

"It's delicious."

"I'm glad you like it," Mistorm answered with a grin.

Tisse turned her attention to the old hero of Zoltan. "The stray assassin I fought gave up the client who had hired them to kill you."

"""What?"""

Both Mistorm and I were shocked at that.

"It was Admiral Lilinrala of the Veronian navy."

"Ahh, so she's responsible." There was a mix of surprise and understanding on Mistorm's face.

Tisse looked a bit unsure whether to continue, but she did regardless. "The stray assassin also revealed who you used to be."

Mistorm took a breath and exhaled before nodding. "If it's come to that, then I see no reason to hide it from you any longer."

"Thank you."

Tisse looked relieved. She was particularly close to Mistorm, more so than the rest of us. I'm sure being caught between not wanting to keep secrets from us and not wanting to out Mistorm without permission had been stressful.

Mistorm smiled kindly to see Tisse so allayed.

"It may have only been for a short while, but we all traveled together as comrades, and I apologize for making you worry for me. However, I wasn't trying to deceive you. As far as I'm concerned, Mistorm is my real name. I've been called that far longer than anything else."

True. She had arrived in Zoltan in her late twenties. Mistorm had been her identity for over forty years. Even if it was an alias at first, it had long since become her real name.

Eventually, the same thing would happen to me, too. There would come a day when I had lived as Red longer than Gideon. Seeing the look on Mistorm's face, I got the feeling that wouldn't be such a bad thing.

"So then, what is your old name?" Rit asked.

"I was previously known as Misphia, wife of King Geizeric and the First Queen of Veronia. I was also called the Pirate Princess Misphia, captain of the Geizeric Pirates' second ship."

It wasn't that crazy of a story that the queen who had disappeared had ended up in Zoltan, home to all runaways. But even if it wasn't unexpected, it was still surprising.

Mistorm appeared to enjoy the look on our faces.

"Well then, where should I start?" Mistorm wondered aloud.

"How about from the beginning?" Yarandrala suggested.

I turned to the high elf. "Do you already know what's going on, Yarandrala?"

"More or less. Truthfully, I'm not entirely unrelated."

"Really? But you didn't have any contact with Mistorm when she was queen, right?"

If she had, they would have recognized each other when they first met in Zoltan.

"Not directly. But I knew Geizeric and Lilinrala."

"You did?"

"It's not like they were particularly close friends. I met Lilinrala when she was a navigator for an exploration vessel. I was the first mate at the time. My blessing isn't particularly useful out on the seas, but it is still part of the Druid tree, so I can sense ocean spirits."

"Huh, I never pictured you sailing the seas," I admitted.

"Who hasn't dreamt of riding the waves in search of an adventure?" Yarandrala replied.

"Fair enough… Still, you've really done a lot."

Yarandrala grinned proudly at my comment. "I've had a bit of a long life after all!"

I'd heard a few of her tales, of course, but it seemed there were far more. Just how much questing had she done?

"Anyway, one day, when we fought off some pirates who attacked our ship, Lilinrala stole one of their vessels and made off with it."

"Was there any reason?"

"At the time, there were uprisings and revolutions all across the continent. A lot of people were captured during the conflicts and sold into slavery. High elves sold particularly well, and Lilinrala couldn't abide that. She became a pirate captain herself and went after every slave ship she could.

Naturally, she didn't sell anyone she rescued, but that meant caring for them. It wasn't long until her funds ran dry. Left with no other choice, she turned to stealing from merchant boats, too, and eventually became a fierce buccaneer who would rob good and honest people," Yarandrala recounted.

Mistorm looked particularly interested in the high elf's story. "You don't say. She never really talked much about her past. So that's how she ended up becoming a pirate."

"I couldn't stand her turning to a life of crime and causing problems for everyone! So I got my hands on a ship myself and fought it out with her and the Elven Corsairs!"

"That's totally like you," I said. That intensity was definitely one of the sides of Yarandrala. She was the sort you didn't want to make an enemy of. "Is that how you met Geizeric?"

"Geizeric was a slave on one of the ships Lilinrala raided. I couldn't tell you why, but she took an interest in him."

I raised an eyebrow. "He was a slave? That's a pretty rough start to life."

"Yes. It was bad enough that Lilinrala sent me a letter requesting a temporary ceasefire because a boy she had picked up was on the verge of death. I felt bad, so I sent some medicine to help," Yarandrala explained.

So then Yarandrala had saved Geizeric, too, in a way.

"Geizeric became a member of Lilinrala's crew and eventually struck out on his own as a pirate. I would never have guessed he'd get big enough to steal a country, though.

Before he made a name for himself, the frost giants started to invade Kiramin, so I sold my ship and formed a band of mercenaries to help. After that, I never had any contact with them again."

"Wait, so you led a band of mercenaries into war? I've been through more than my fair share as a knight and a member of the Hero's party, but your life was crazy tumultuous when you were young," I said.

"Eh-heh-heh." Yarandrala blushed like she thought that was a compliment. "Anyway, if I had defeated Lilinrala and Geizeric, Mistorm's life would have been completely different. So it feels like I'm partly responsible for all this."

"Life's an odd thing. Just when I thought I had reached a nice age and all that remained was to wait for Lord Demis to call me home, new faces and old friends started to pop up and throw me for a loop." Mistorm's expression appeared very conflicted. However, if I had to guess, I'd say she mostly felt thankful.

* * *

Rit nodded to herself. "Okay, we understand your connection. So now we can get to the crux of the matter."

"I assume you mean why they're after me," Mistorm replied as she set down her empty cup.

"Prince Salius is searching for you, right?"

"I've no way of knowing for sure, but I believe that's the case." Mistorm stopped for a moment to shrug. "One option might be to just give it up and turn myself in for Zoltan's sake."

"Mistorm!" Yarandrala fired back sharply.

I thought for a moment before continuing. "But if he's looking for you, then why does Lilinrala want you dead?"

"Yeah," Rit added with a bitter sort of face. "Lilinrala acts as a loyal vassal to Prince Salius, but their goals are clearly at odds."

"That's right. Prince Salius is desperate enough to find you that he's pressuring the holy church, yet those assassins knew where you were and what you looked like," I said, fixing my gaze on Mistorm. She met my eyes and gave a slow exhale.

"Before I say more, I'd like to ask, just how deeply do you intend to get involved?"

"You're a friend who traveled with us all the way to the Wall at the End of the World. If you're in danger, we're prepared to assist," I answered.

"That's the exact same thing Yarandrala said. Sheesh, it was just one little trip... Perhaps that's simply how adventurers are. Seems I've been retired long enough to forget."

Mistorm looked away and then smiled a little.

"All right then, I guess it's time for an old story."

Interlude

The Story of the Exiled Queen Misphia

Fifty years ago, in the Veronian royal palace, a young Mistorm—Princess Misphia—was wearing a beautiful dress, dancing in the hall's center. Her escort was a blond young man draped in resplendent aristocratic attire. His elegant manner garnered the attention of everyone around.

As the dance drew to a close, the young man disappeared, called away by a butler.

"Oh, sister."

Now that Misphia's dance had concluded, another girl was approaching her. There was a resemblance between the two, but the other young woman's eyes were gentler. Misphia's beauty was the sort to be renowned far and wide, but the other girl's was more the beauty of a flower beloved by all.

"Leonor," Misphia greeted.

"Lord Pietro is a marvelous dancer, don't you think? It's always such a pleasure to dance with him," Leonor said.

"He surely is, although a bit lacking in resolution. As a member of a side branch of the royal family, it would be better for him to maintain a tad more gravity when dealing with other nobles."

"Even on days like this, you never forget yourself. A woman's role is to raise her man up, is it not?"

"If a successor is not born to Father, then Lord Pietro will ascend to the throne. What Veronia needs now is a strong king. Is it not the job of a good wife to support and guide her husband?"

"Oh my! To envision your husband becoming king! Such ambition, sister." Leonor raised her voice slightly as she spoke, causing nearby aristocrats to glance over. "Ah, my apologies," Leonor said softly, but her expression was twisted with malicious satisfaction. "I suppose that aspiration befits a mighty Archmage. A mere Fighter like myself could never hope to compare. I'm quite content with my blessing, however. After all, flowers exist to be admired. The inherent skills of Fighter are simple physical enhancement, and its impulses are minor. Few blessings would allow one to devote herself to beauty so wholeheartedly."

"I would much prefer being a simple herb that cures disease than a hothouse flower to be ogled," Misphia responded resolutely.

Leonor smirked behind the fan she held in her hand.

"How splendid. It truly is a joy to chat with you, Big Sister. The thought of you leaving the palace is so heart-wrenching."

"I would have liked to be able to share so many more things with you as well," Misphia responded.

The king of Veronia rose on stage. Apparently, there was an announcement to make. Pietro was standing next to him. The nobles around the platform applauded.

"As king of Veronia and as your sovereign leader, I am pleased to celebrate this joyous day with you," the king began, and there was another round of clapping.

Misphia watched with a mix of joy and melancholy. However, things quickly took an unexpected turn.

"You who support our beloved Veronia, I asked you here on this day to bear witness to the vows binding our beloved and faithful retainer, Pietro de Zaqui, and my beloved daughter Leonor of Veronia."

Silence filled the room but was quickly broken by many troubled whispers.

"M-my lord… Lady Leonor? Not Lady Misphia?"

"Yes. I did not misspeak. Pietro and Leonor."

Misphia looked on, unable to believe what was happening, but when she saw Pietro's innocent smile as he stepped up onto the stage, she realized what had happened. Her face paled, and she clenched her fists.

"And…"

A man named Duke Oslo stepped onto the platform, and the Veronian nobles looked away.

"My m-my most trusted Duke Oslo has great regard for my daughter Misphia's talent."

The king's voice trembled in mortification that he could not entirely hide. Sweat formed on his brow, and his eyes were bloodshot. As the ruler of the Kingdom of Veronia, that was all he was permitted in protest while praises for Duke Oslo poured from his mouth. "I ask that all might share in my joy at Duke Oslo taking my daughter Misphia as his bride. Today is truly blessed."

"B-but, Your Highness, Duke Oslo already has a wife," an older noble nervously interjected.

Those around him all nodded.

Duke Oslo answered in the king's stead, his blackened teeth showing beneath his smirk.

"I am delighted to welcome Lady Misphia as a concubine."

Unwilling to stand by, the older noble loudly objected. "That's absurd! Lady Misphia is the first princess of the Veronian royal family! E-even for a duke, that is an outrage…"

"What's the problem?"

Duke Oslo nodded in satisfaction, not even bothering with an excuse, leaving the old noble dumbfounded.

Other aristocrats were struck by a sinking feeling that this spelled the end of their kingdom. At present, Veronia was a reasonably powerful country, but that hadn't been the case only fifty years prior.

Later, Misphia sat defeated and alone in her room when Leonor came by. Her eyes shone with the thrill of victory.

"Congratulations on your betrothal. May your marriage be long and happy, young herb."

* * *

Seagulls cried as they glided past the ship.

The vessel used for Misphia's bridal procession was a single-masted old-style sailing boat. Duke Oslo's emissary had come on the rough, humble ship to greet Princess Misphia. The boat creaked as it rolled with the waves, gently rocking the room.

Misphia was wearing an expensive white dress and gazing down at the floor of her guest cabin in misery.

Nothing assuaged the humiliation of becoming Duke Oslo's concubine. If it had been for the sake of her country, then Misphia would have endured it. But this decision had only marred Veronia's reputation. It had done nothing but reveal to the world how weak the nation had become.

The great Veronia, once a rival to Avalonia, was not long for this world. Surely, that thought was on everyone's minds. Misphia did her best not to cry, biting her lip to keep her heart from breaking.

"Please... Someone save us."

No sooner had the words left her mouth than a sudden clamor erupted outside. Shouts came from all over, accompanied by the clanging of metal. Sensing something was amiss, Misphia grabbed her staff, which stood in the corner of the room. Not long after, the door flew open.

"Hohhh."

A man entered. His face was covered in scars, his gaze sharp and piercing. A confident expression bloomed on his face. He was a man of an entirely different sort from the Veronian nobles Misphia was familiar with.

"Seems I've found the greatest treasure on the ship."

"What business do you have here, pirate? You dare perpetrate this villainy knowing that a member of the royal family was on this vessel?!"

"Royal family, huh? Hah, what power is there in a royal family who would sell their princess off as a concubine to a mere duke?" the pirate spat, sneering.

"Silence!" Misphia's face turned red in humiliation. "I will return Veronia to its glory days. If I must stain myself in shame to do so, fine! Duke Oslo's estate is powerful. If he takes an interest in me and some of my children are able to inherit some of that land..."

"There's no chance of that for a concubine. He's just a lecherous old man. Duke Oslo doesn't give a shit about that sort of gallantry. All he cares about is..." The pirate approached Misphia and poked her breast.

"Eeek!" Misphia covered her chest with both hands.

"That."

Misphia glared at the man. He whistled in response.

"Is it really so bad to be a concubine? You can live in luxury."

"I'm a princess. I live and die for the sake of my country. That is why I was born!"

"That's a pretty bold way to put it."

"As if a thief could ever comprehend."

The pirate grinned. "Well, as it happens, I've got an interest in how royals live. So, how about it? Why not teach me about your way of life?"

"What...?"

"You are the greatest treasure of any I've seen. Giving you back to some duke would be a waste."

"Eeek!"

"I'll be taking you. I am a pirate, after all."

"U-unhand me!"

"Don't worry, you won't have to give up on your dream… Because I'll become king."

"King…? What are you talking about…?"

"I've got the Divine Blessing of the Emperor. That rarest of blessings the first Avalonian king was said to have had."

Geizeric took Misphia's hand and opened the door out of the room.

The sea breeze filled her lungs.

"My name is Geizeric! I have no last name, and I have never met my parents. I am Geizeric and nothing more! But I will become the king of Veronia!"

"Um…"

"Princess! I want you to be my right hand! Teach this pirate what it means to be a king! In exchange, I will raise Veronia such that no worthless noble can steal its princesses ever again!"

The Pirate Emperor Geizeric, the future king of Veronia, took Misphia's arm in his strong grasp and began to walk. At first, Misphia staggered a bit, but soon she was able to follow behind him with sure steps on her own two feet. The pair left the cramped room on the ship and walked out into the wide open.

The Divine Blessing of the Emperor. The blessing that the first ruler of Avalonia supposedly possessed. It was even rarer than the Hero.

Avalonians were said to be descended from the vassals of aristocrats who had been cast out by the ruler of Gaiapolis, the son of a previous Hero.

At the time, the land that would become Avalonia was undeveloped and wild. The first king was a champion who gathered people, developed the untamed region, battled monsters, and established a new kingdom.

In a world where one's blessing determined one's life, Geizeric had been born for the throne.

*　　　*　　　*

"I'll split it evenly, so don't go filching any!"

"Aye aye, miss!"

Misphia had changed from a dress to a buccaneer's outfit that was easier to move in. Magic staff in hand, she was giving orders to the pirates. Her staff was different from the old one she'd wielded. This new rod had a narrow and sharp metal point, allowing it to be handled like a spear. She even wore a scabbard at her hip for sheathing the staff.

At Misphia's orders, the pirates started carrying back their plunder from the enemy vessel.

"She's gotten mighty comfortable with things," remarked a one-eyed high elf standing beside Geizeric.

"This is Ms. Lilinrala," Geizeric introduced to Misphia.

"Cut the 'Ms.' crap. I'm just Lilinrala."

Misphia beheld the grinning pair, and the tan young woman quickly found herself smiling as well.

* * *

Geizeric's crew had attacked a western port on the dark continent that was filled with dwarves and orcs. The area was rife with armor, weapons, and monsters that were unheard of on the continent of Avalon.

Odd weapons like a thin-bladed, whip-like sword, a mechanical hammer that worked by setting off an alchemic explosive powder to fire an anchor bolt, a giant's skull attached to a chain, or a dwarven mechanical bow that fired arrows one after the other simply by pulling a trigger.

The pirates sated themselves with combat, running around and cheering as they carried off treasures.

And as Geizeric escaped to the seas in his boat, several shadows leaped into the air to follow.

"Hard starboard and full speed ahead!" Geizeric shouted.

Gandor of the Wind's elite wyvern knights were flying through the skies.

"Cap'n! Maybe we shouldn't have tried to steal loot from the demon lord's army!"

"What's a pirate doin' getting scared of some demon lord!"

There was a brilliant flash and thunderous boom at their backs.

"Uwaaaah!"

One pirate shouted as another ship was sent to the bottom of the ocean by a streak of lightning.

"A Storm Javelin spell?! Who did that?!"

"Me."

A white-haired wind demon astride a wyvern looked down at the pirates with a bolt of electricity in its hands.

"One of Gandor's kin! We created enough trouble for an upper-tier demon general to show up!" Lilinrala shouted.

She had lost her own boat during the fighting, so she had come aboard Geizeric's.

The demon summoned another crackling spear.

"Your ship is quite the relic. Did you steal it from a museum? Are you an outcast of the plains people? Whatever could have possessed you to attack our warehouse?"

"Who asked you?! No pirate worth their salt would turn their back on plunder just sitting there in front of them!" Geizeric shot back.

"You call yourself a pirate with a boat like that? Incomprehensible. It matters not. You'll be dying here."

"D-dammit! Quit floating around up there! Get down here and face me like a man!" Geizeric shouted, waving his saber.

The wind demon showed no signs of acquiescing. Instead, it hurled more Storm Javelins down.

"Wind Control!"

Misphia formed a seal and activated her magic. The air shrouding the Storm Javelin dissipated unnaturally, flowing into a powerful tailwind in the ship's sails.

"What?!" For the first time, the demon's confident expression cracked.

A Storm Javelin tracked its target, and Misphia's intermediate arcane magic spell Wind Control wasn't enough to stop it. Knowing this, she had instead used her power to push the boat.

As the spear of lightning drew closer, the ship would accelerate in response. The boat and javelins moved in tandem, quickly leaving the demons behind.

"Yahooo!" Geizeric cheered. Unfortunately, the gale carrying the boat was rapidly growing too intense. The masts were starting to bend and creak.

"Cap'n! The ship can't take it! She's gonna break!" one of the pirates called out, on the verge of tears.

However, Geizeric just grinned and kicked the mast, laughing off his crew's worries.

"She ain't gonna break! If she wants to call herself my ship, she'll show her guts!"

"Don't be absurd," Misphia responded, astonished.

"Bein' a pirate means doin' the absurd day in and day out! Ga-ha-ha-ha!"

"I…can't argue with that."

Despite the perilous situation, or perhaps because of it, Misphia and Geizeric laughed together.

"I was plannin' to get you to teach me how to act like a proper king, but looks like you learned how to be a proper buccaneer first!"

"And whose fault do you think that is? You better take responsibility."

Geizeric's grin widened at that remark.

Chapter 4

Conflicting Goals

Mistorm seemed to be enjoying herself as she regaled us with the story of her early years.

"We rampaged all around the dark continent's coasts. In the end, we stole the demon lord's ship and returned to Veronia."

"What happened next?" Rit urged her to keep going.

Mistorm's tale was both a romance of a cast-out princess meeting a pirate and an epic adventure that spanned the world. To Rit, it must have seemed an exciting tale.

"The demon lord's ship employed technology unknown to Avalon. It was an enormous iron battleship that used steam and magic to move. Duke Oslo couldn't hope to match us when we returned with it. It was around that time that the goblin king was causing panic all across Veronia. In exchange for helping maintain the peace, Geizeric was made a noble."

I knew what came next from history. With the army at his command, Geizeric led a coup d'état and defeated Mistorm's father, the king of Veronia.

"I still see it sometimes in my dreams."

Mistorm closed her eyes.

* * *

Pirates kicked open the door to the throne room.

"Misphia! You are my daughter and a princess! You would bring the royal line to ruin?!" exclaimed the king.

Misphia did not falter, however, standing firmly by Geizeric's side.

"Father, a nation must be strong. Royalty who are only used by degenerate nobles like Duke Oslo, who lose over half of their lands from repeated defeats, and who can't even protect their villages from the goblin king… What value is there in royalty who cling to their crumbling authority and bicker among themselves?"

"And what would you have me do?! I am ruler in name only! I inherited a pitiful royal army that could not best mere bands of thieves and retainers who embezzled from the treasury with impunity! What could anyone do in that situation?!"

"That complacency is your sin! Rather than lamenting the incompetents around you, you should have helped those who relied on the royal family!" Misphia roared, denouncing her parent.

The king of Veronia hung his head, crestfallen.

"I take it you know what you must do, then."

"Yes."

Misphia's father looked to Geizeric, the next Veronian king.

"You are strong, wise, and brave, Geizeric—wholly unlike myself."

"…"

"I have but one thing to say to you… Show no mercy."

"What?"

"Should you leave even one member of the royal family alive, people will rally to them and resist. If you would be king, you must show no mercy. Benevolence breeds revenge. Magnanimity leads to blood. That is what it means to rule."

Misphia's father drew his sword and held it to his neck.

"Geizeric, is it true that you possess the Divine Blessing of the Emperor?"

"Yes."

"Then this is only natural. How enviable. Do you know my Divine Blessing?"

"No, Misphia told me she never learned it, either."

"Indeed. Because it's not something to be shared widely. Only a select few were ever informed. My Divine Blessing is Herbalist. From the start, I was ill-suited to the life of a ruler… I would have rather sold medicine in a small apothecary."

A sad smile crossed the man's lips as he closed his eyes, pressed the sword to his neck, and thrust.

The royal aides screamed. Geizeric closed his eyes in a brief show of respect for the dead king. Heeding the late man's advice, he then slaughtered everyone still left alive.

* * *

"But we didn't kill Leonor," Mistorm said.

"The other princess of Veronia, huh?" I knew Queen Leonor. And the mention of her brought back an unpleasant memory.

Noticing my expression, Rit asked, "Red?" She looked concerned.

"No, it's nothing." I shook my head, urging Mistorm to continue.

I trusted Mistorm, but there was no need for me to say that I had met her sibling.

"My younger sister… Leonor immediately turned over her husband Pietro to Geizeric and pledged her loyalty to us. What would the remaining nobles think if we killed someone who had surrendered? If they believed conceding wasn't enough to earn mercy and forgiveness, then they would've had no choice but to fight to the last. Our forces had overwhelmed all of the aristocrats, but if the fighting dragged on, other countries might get involved, sensing opportunity. To quell the chaos as quickly as possible, there was no alternative but to send Leonor to a convent."

Mistorm smiled wryly.

"The best choice would probably have been to have her assassinated in the cloister once everything was over. Ahh, but I was naïve. Father was right. In the end, I was forced to leave, and Leonor took the seat next to King Geizeric."

"What? But there was more between you and Geizeric than just personal gain! He loved you, didn't he?!" Rit argued, unable to accept it.

Mistorm shook her head.

"Geizeric's blessing is Emperor. His role is to be ruler. That doesn't end with taking the throne. He needed a son—a prince—who would inherit both Geizeric's blood and that of the previous royal lineage. Geizeric was an upstart, self-made noble who began as a pirate. He required something to legitimize his offspring."

"Then why not you…?" Rit questioned.

"Three children stillborn. I nearly died with them… I couldn't bear to see my babies so terribly silent."

Sorrowful tears formed in Rit's eyes.

No… Wait a second! I thought, realizing something.

"Isn't Prince Salius your child? He dropped in the line of succession because his mother—you—went missing, right?"

"And that is the root of the problem plaguing Zoltan. The mistake Lilinrala and I made."

"You don't mean he's…"

"He isn't my son. Salius is a child whom Lilinrala brought in when my third baby was born dead. He was an orphan with the same colored hair and eyes as Geizeric."

If word of that got out, it would shake Veronia to its foundation.

"Geizeric had already taken Leonor into his harem at that point, because he desperately needed a child who would carry on the previous royal line. If Leonor had gotten pregnant first, Lilinrala and the faction who remained from our pirating days would have been in danger."

"So Lilinrala was disloyal to Geizeric," Yarandrala stated, visibly indignant. To a high elf, betraying someone was more shameful than anything. She couldn't accept the choice Lilinrala had made.

"She didn't have any other option," Mistorm defended.

"I look away for a few years, and she forgets what it means to be a high elf," Yarandrala hissed. "I should have finished her off when she became a pirate."

She was furious.

"I understand your feelings, Yarandrala, but please don't go charging out to her ship to take her on, okay?" I entreated.

"Mrgh." She crossed her arms and growled.

"Really, I'm begging you here!"

Yarandrala really looked like she wanted to go on a rampage…

"I can't forgive King Geizeric for being so heartless!" Rit shouted abruptly. "No matter how strong the impulses, letting Mistorm's most bitter enemy into his bed is unforgivable!"

"I get it, but there's not much point in arguing with Mistorm," I replied.

"If it were me, I wouldn't consider anyone other than you," Rit fired back. I had no idea how to reply to that.

"Look, let's not get too far off the topic, all right?" I said clumsily.

Mistorm laughed at my reaction.

"Yes, yes, let's continue the story." It must have been a painful subject to revisit, but the old woman's expression didn't appear troubled. Her time in Zoltan had turned her experiences in Veronia into just memories. "I've already covered the biggest point about Prince Salius and Lilinrala's relationship. Other than that…"

"Could you tell us why you left Veronia? Your positions should have been protected with the replacement prince Lilinrala found," I stated.

"I don't know how she caught wind of it, but Leonor knew about Salius and threatened me, demanding that I disappear. At the time, I was totally broken. I had resigned myself to the idea that Lilinrala and I would be executed, but Salius was innocent. Even if he wouldn't be king, I still wanted him to live in peace."

"And that's why you did as Leonor instructed?"

"Yes, I left Veronia without saying a word. That allowed Leonor to become Geizeric's true wife and her children rose above Salius in the line of succession."

Mistorm was yet another cast-out who had found her way to Zoltan.

"I see. Now it all makes sense."

Naturally, I had my opinions about Mistorm's life, but the priority was resolving the issue at hand.

There was no doubt that Prince Salius and his Veronian forces were searching for Mistorm. They knew they were searching for someone with an Archmage blessing who would've arrived in Zoltan roughly forty-five years ago, so finding Mistorm in the holy church's records would be a simple task. Mistorm's blessing was rare and high-level—there was no one in Zoltan with one like it. Prince Salius presumably hoped to locate Mistorm and return her to Veronia to reclaim his position as primary candidate for the throne.

It was a dangerous path to tread, but if he wanted to advance himself, there was little alternative.

"But Lilinrala's goal is different."

She didn't want Mistorm returning to Veronia. Her aim was to eliminate the old woman before Prince Salius could make contact with her.

"She's probably worried that Leonor will reveal the truth about Prince Salius if you come back," I said.

"That's what I think, too, though I can't say for sure," Mistorm agreed.

"Demanding the holy church's registers to find you without revealing that he's searching for a queen. It makes sense on the surface, but most everyone in Zoltan knows the Archmage Mistorm. Prince Salius should've discovered who you were rather quickly."

"True," Rit replied, nodding. "That's something you could figure out by looking into normal records. You wouldn't even have to ask around."

"Let's see if we can make sense of this, then. What if the prince received a report that the queen might be in Zoltan, so he ordered Lilinrala to find her? Lilinrala panicked, however, because finding the queen could ruin both her and the prince," I suggested. It certainly explained why she'd chosen a more indirect method. "After buying herself time, Lilinrala sent those stray assassins to kill Mistorm."

"Everything starts to make sense when you put it that way," Rit said.

"Well, aren't you something?" Mistorm shook her head in amazement. "So long as you're in Zoltan, I can retire without worry."

I smiled a bit at that. She had said the same thing to Ruti as well. Feeling like I was comparable to Ruti nearly made me blush.

"All right. So now it's a question of what to do next," I stated.

"Mhm."

"I'll report back to Ruti, and then my job here will be done." Resolving everything wasn't my job here. It'd be fine to entrust things to my sister.

"Hah, I see, I see. You're better at this than I was," Mistorm commented with a laugh. "As mayor, I tried to solve everything myself. With someone like you around, Zoltan's future looks bright."

"I've got no intention of becoming mayor," I replied.

"That's okay. You need only do what you believe is best for your home. If everyone follows that creed, things will be fine. While I knew that myself, I still couldn't help but try to solve issues on my own in my younger days."

It sounded like Mistorm still had a few regrets from her time as mayor.

"You're all good as you are. I can't wait to see the sort of Zoltan you build."

Mistorm appeared to be in fair spirits, but Rit and I both understood the underlying feeling. She believed that Zoltan was in good hands without her, so she could turn herself over to Lilinrala if the situation began to look like it would take a turn for the worse.

"I don't want that," Rit whispered to me.

"Yeah, me neither," I responded quietly. After collecting myself, I said, "All right, that's all for the conversation regarding Mistorm. Now Rit and I should take care of our original goal."

Yarandrala cocked her head. "Your original goal?"

With all the excitement, I'd nearly forgotten about it myself, but we had originally wanted to consult Yarandrala about harvesting coconuts.

"I was hoping to get your advice on something." I started to explain the situation to Yarandrala. Mistorm smiled, evidently enjoying herself as she listened.

* * *

With the discussion finished, we all took a break.

The sun had begun to sink into the horizon, so the plan was to stay the night here and head back to Zoltan in the morning.

Mistorm's house had been scorched in the fighting, but Tisse and Mister Crawly Wawly were helping the old people of the village to clean it up.

"Queen Leonor, huh?" I muttered.

Rit and I were relaxing in the guest room.

"There are a lot of nasty rumors about her," Rit noted.

"She's at the center of the pro-demon lord's army faction in Veronia. Some nobles in Avalonia call her an enemy of humanity."

Rit rested her chin on her palm. "An enemy of humanity… Most people in Loggervia hate her, too, since she's the architect of Veronia's non-aggression pact with the demon lord's armies."

"You'd be hard-pressed to find anyone who thought well of her in Avalonia," I stated.

"But is that really all there is to her? I mean, there's no mistaking she's a terrible woman—she drove Mistorm out of Veronia, after all. But there are different levels of evil."

An old memory came to mind, and I grimaced. "Yeah, about that."

"By any chance, have you met her before?" Rit questioned. She must have noticed my expression.

"I have. Before I was knighted, when I was still a squire."

Few non-Veronians had laid eyes on Queen Leonor. She was the type of queen who focused more on dealing with the aristocrats of her own country and didn't take the foreign stage. The best way to describe it might've been to compare her to Lilinrala. One led the navy, and the other controlled the land-holding vassals.

Six years ago, I had gone to Veronia with the old knight I served.

Our mission was one of diplomacy and investigation.

At the time, the conflict between Veronia and Avalonia had died down some, and we were moving toward reconciliation. The chief diplomat of Veronia favored mutual peace, and my knight master was negotiating with him. Thus, I was tasked with investigating the situation in Veronia and reporting back. My work was proceeding smoothly when I ran into her.

"She looked like a doll. I couldn't imagine her being older than a teenager," I described.

Rit gawked. "Huh?! But she's Mistorm's sister, right?! She must have been nearly seventy!"

"Undoubtedly, she used magic and alchemy to mess with her body and maintain her appearance. The method consumes heaps of expensive magical ingredients, however."

I didn't know much about the recipe for maintaining youth beyond that, though. It was a tightly kept secret passed down among a small group of alchemists.

"She concealed her identity and tried to lure me over to Veronia's side. I refused, of course, but..." I trailed off.

"But?" Rit pressed, eager to hear more.

"She was furious. She revealed who she was and broke down the reconciliation talks. Then she ordered the army to hit Avalonia with a surprise attack."

"Negotiations fell apart because she got mad?!" Rit exclaimed.

"Not only that, my superior and I were caught and almost executed," I continued.

"What?! Executing a diplomat?! That would cause a lot more than a minor diplomatic scuffle!"

"I was really nervous. Knowing that a full-on war might break out if we died, we tried desperately to escape. It was awful."

"If Avalonia and Veronia had started fighting, the human kingdoms would have been destroyed in no time once the demon lord's army came," Rit said.

"I only found out later, but Lilinrala had apparently managed to pull the army back at the border. Unfortunately, Leonor just used that to strengthen her own position by spreading rumors that Lilinrala had become a coward in her old age."

"Hmm. I can't tell if she's brilliant or an idiot." Rit was royalty, too—the princess of Loggervia, a nation known for its clashes with its neighbors. Thus, she understood that there were different levels of conflict. She knew that as long as neither side went too far, arguments did not have to end in battle. To Rit, Leonor likely seemed a fool of a queen who nearly started a war over some tantrum.

"Anyway, it's a good thing Leonor won't be coming to Zoltan. She knows who I am, and she's not an easy person to deal with," I remarked.

Rit narrowed her eyes. "So there are enemies even you have trouble dealing with."

"Of course there are. But I was still just a knight in training back then… I'd like to think I could handle things better now."

"I want to hear more about that story later!"

"Sure. We can talk it over after we get back to Zoltan and the situation has calmed down."

I hadn't told Rit much about my time with the knights. It might be nice to reminisce about that with her. I took my bag of medicine and stood.

"Where are you going?" Rit asked.

"I was thinking of having a look at the people living here. I was a little curious before."

"Ah, yeah, it is a hidden village, after all." Rit rose from her seat, too. "Okay, then I'll be Dr. Red's assistant."

"Ha-ha, you know I'm not a doctor."

"Don't sweat the small stuff!"

There was no dissuading her when she got like this. Rit flashed a grin, and seeing her adorable face, I couldn't help smiling back.

After informing Tisse of what we were going to do, Rit and I headed outside. A bird was cawing in the night somewhere. I set my sights on the home I was searching for and knocked politely.

"Just a second." The door opened, and an old woman we had seen when we first came to the village appeared. "Oh, if it isn't the young miss's guests. I heard quite the ruckus earlier. Are you all right?"

"Yes, we're fine, thank you ma'am. If you don't mind me asking, are you having difficulty with your left eye?"

She raised a hand to the spot in question and smiled wryly. "You're quite observant, dear. It has been giving me some trouble."

"I run an apothecary, you see. And I brought some medicine that should help," I said.

"I'd love that, but even the young miss's magic couldn't heal it. Can a common curative really do anything?" the elderly woman inquired.

"It's precisely because it's *not* magic that it can."

Healing spells were convenient, but their effects removed the source of a disease or sickness. Unfortunately, even if the pathogen was removed, magic didn't repair the internal damage caused by that pathogen. That was why it had been so crucial to treat Tanta's white-eye early. Restoring any vision loss would require regeneration magic once the disease had been expunged. There were few people capable of that feat, however. The Archmage blessing that had the ability to remove pathogens couldn't do anything more.

Medicine was different, though. A body that was unable to function properly due to sickness could be restored to some extent by drugs made using herbs and alchemy, though slower than a spell.

"I think the nerves in your eye have been hurt. If I'm not mistaken, your field of vision has narrowed," I explained.

Rit retrieved a small vial out of the bag. I accepted it from her and showed it to the old lady.

"If you use these eye drops, your sight should improve a little, and the medicine will prevent further deterioration. Regretfully, I can't fully cure the issue, but your vision should be as strong as anyone else's for another ten years or so."

"Oooh," the old woman marveled. "Please, come on in. No point standing around chatting."

* * *

"Thank you both for the information. I'd like to buy those drops."

After we had gone over everything, the old woman nodded. She took the medicine that I handed over and gave me forty quarter payrils.

"I'll come by with some more when that starts to run out," I said.

"I'd appreciate that. We don't get any traveling merchants around here, so all we can do is have the young miss buy things we can't make ourselves."

"Is there no doctor in the village?" Rit asked.

The old woman shook her head. "We used to have old man Ruy, the ship's doctor...but he's sailing new seas in his next life now."

"I see."

"Oh, since you're here, could you perhaps take a look at the others? There's no one but us old folks here, and we've all got some wear and tear."

"Sure," I answered. "I was planning to visit everyone. And I'll be sure to come by once a month to sell medicine, too."

"In that case, it may be easier to gather everyone here. A few folks are bedridden, however. If you could examine them when you're done, that would be lovely," the old woman said.

"Got it. I've got the time, so we'll make sure everyone receives the care they need."

With that, I set to work diagnosing villagers, selling curatives I had on hand, and taking orders for my next visit.

* * *

Speaking with all the villages and visiting those who couldn't leave their homes ended up taking quite a while.

"Thanks for your help, Rit. I've got plenty of experience tending to wounded people, but dealing with the troubles of the elderly has its unique challenges."

"No problem. I only did what you told me to, though. My knowledge ends at the basic first aid stuff I picked up as an adventurer."

"Your assistance allowed me to focus on providing the best care. Seriously, thank you, Rit."

"Heh-heh."

"It was a lot of effort, but we sold a pretty good amount of medicine. Handling an entire village's needs will be good for our sales," I commented.

After discovering a new group of customers, Rit and I were in high spirits. As we were walking together, Rit suddenly asked, "Do you remember the sales numbers I calculated when we started out?"

"Of course. The day we reunited in Zoltan is an important one to me."

"...Our sales since then have been much, much better than I would ever have guessed. You really are amazing, Red."

"It's only because you've been by my side through it all. It wouldn't have gone nearly as smoothly without you."

I wouldn't have solved Zoltan's oil problem were it not for Rit. My successes were all because of her guidance.

"Thank you, Red. I'm glad I could support you."

"You know, I often wonder how to repay you," I admitted.

"Being yours is enough."

We were whispering to each other, our shoulders touching as we walked. As we approached Mistorm's house, we noticed Bishop Shien standing out in front.

"Thank you for your hard work, Red, Rit." He had a gentle smile as he greeted us.

"Bishop Shien, how's that wound feeling?" I inquired.

"I still feel a little bit sluggish. I guess I can't be as reckless as I was in my youth." He chuckled wryly. "You two have been examining the locals, right? You have my gratitude."

The man who stood at the head of Zoltan's holy church bowed

deeply in a show of appreciation for two humble apothecaries. I was at a loss for words, in shock. He raised his head to show that he was grinning.

"Because of Mistorm's secret, we couldn't tell others about this village. Still, it hurt to know that we were forcing heroes who once saved Zoltan to live in such an inconvenient situation. I'm truly appreciative."

"Ah, they're the Veronian pirates who came with Mistorm, then?" I said.

"Yes. Each is a champion who safeguarded Zoltan from the shadows."

Comrades from when Mistorm had sailed with Geizeric. They had given up everything to follow Mistorm when she could no longer stay in Veronia and had remained by her side to this day.

"They really idolize her."

"Naturally. Apparently, Mistorm kicked Geizeric and the rest of the crew into action when she joined. The ship was teeming with mold, making it an awful place to live. Mistorm was the one who got them to clean. She did research and worked with the ship's cook to prepare foods necessary for long journeys. Honestly, it sounds like she did it all. Get any one of these old timers a drink, and they'll always talk about how 'the young miss was the best captain.'"

I smiled at the thought of Princess Misphia transforming into Mistorm sailing the seas. It must have been a never-ending series of culture shocks.

"You know… I can hold my own in a fight well enough, but it seems that heroes are often hidden in plain sight," Bishop Shien commented. "Just who are you, Red? Your sister, too, for that matter."

"I'm just a simple shopkeeper running a little apothecary, and my younger sister is just an up-and-coming medicinal herb farmer."

"It was tasteless of me to ask. My apologies," Bishop Shien replied, closing his eyes and putting his hands together. "That you would be in Zoltan during its hour of need can only be the work of Lord Demis. I'm eternally grateful."

The Lord Demis's work, huh? I thought. If this really was God's plan, it was a pretty twisted one.

I laughed awkwardly to myself at that thought, but I understood this had nothing to do with any deity's intentions. It was Ruti, Rit, Tisse, and I. We were here because of our choices, not Demis's.

Chapter 5

Wolf Rit and a Moonlit Night

On the morning of the following day, we left the secluded village.

Three of the riding drakes were gone, so Bishop Shien took the one left, Rit and Tisse rode the spirit dire wolf that Rit summoned, and I ran alongside.

I didn't want people to see me moving this swiftly, so Rit used her Aspect of Wolf to confirm there was no one else nearby.

We reached Zoltan before noon. Rit and I stopped at home to change out of our dirty clothes and then went to see Ruti.

"Welcome back, Big Brother."

For some reason, Ruti was sitting in the mayor's seat. The actual mayor, Tornado, was beside her, where the secretary would normally be, quietly going through paperwork.

What's going on?

"I had to ask Ms. Ruhr for instructions on so many things that it was easier for her to deal with issues first while I followed up and verified things afterward," Mayor Tornado explained with a smile.

"You didn't have to change seats, though," I said.

"This building has been designed to run with the person in the mayor's chair at its heart. The secretary's seat and the mayor's are beside each other, but it makes the most sense that I sit here for now." Tornado gathered up his paperwork and stood.

"I imagine you've got something private to discuss. I can step out."

"No, I'd like you to be here for it as well," Ruti stated, stopping the mayor.

"I see. In that case, I'll join you," Tornado replied before sitting down again.

He was clearly doing his best to make it easier for Ruti to act, but he wasn't blindly entrusting everything to her, either. Mayor Tornado was considering what was best while supporting Ruti.

My respect for him grew a little when I realized that. In terms of political ability, Tornado was undoubtedly not as skilled as Prince Salius or Lilinrala, but he was honest with himself about what he could and couldn't do and always gave careful thought to what was necessary.

If you asked me, the fact that he was mayor was as much a blessing as Ruti's presence in Zoltan. And Ruti appeared to agree.

Zoltan was a small frontier region without any military or economic might, but there were all sorts of people here.

"Prince Salius is looking for Mistorm...," Rit divulged.

Ruti nodded quietly. The mayor's face turned red and then paled in shock. He wiped the sweat that was forming on his brow with his handkerchief.

He certainly gave the impression of being unreliable. Still, he remained where he was and listened to the end.

It was natural for strong people not to run, but the mayor was a small-time, backwater politician. This was a battle far beyond his capabilities, yet he held his ground.

Zoltan was a good place. It was fortunate I'd chosen to settle down here.

"What do you think we should do, Big Brother?" Ruti asked once she'd heard everything.

"About that… If Zoltan is going to protect Mistorm, then I think it would be best to negotiate with Lilinrala," I responded.

"Mhm. I agree. Lilinrala aims to keep Prince Salius and Mistorm from meeting, which is at odds with the prince's goal of taking Mistorm back to Veronia," said Ruti.

I nodded. "If negotiations proceed smoothly, it should be possible to keep both sides from getting hurt."

"But it will be hard to move quickly. If the secret gets out, Lilinrala will move to get rid of everyone with any connection to it," my sister remarked.

"Yeah, that's pretty likely… In that case, why not just wait and watch for a little longer?" I suggested.

"Having lost her subordinates and the stray assassins, she should be getting impatient. It won't be long before she makes a move herself," Ruti stated.

"Let her take her best shot if she wants," Rit declared.

The first lesson of the sword was not to fear being cut—to have the will to take a hit and still win.

"Mistorm's existence isn't a weakness for Zoltan; it's a strength. Both Prince Salius and Lilinrala are bound by her being here. So if we wait, they'll have to make a move," I said.

"Mhm, let's do that." Ruti bobbed her head in agreement, apparently pleased that I was thinking along the same lines as her.

"So we won't be handing Master Mistorm over, then… Thank goodness…" Mayor Tornado looked relieved after hearing Ruti's verdict.

* * *

An emergency the following morning had Ruti hurrying to see me.

I quickly changed, and we took off together toward her farm.

"Red," Tisse called, waving from beside their greenhouse.

It was clear from her eyes that the situation wasn't a pleasant one. Ruti and I went into the greenhouse.

"What should we do, Big Brother...?"

She grabbed my sleeve anxiously. There was no trace of the girl fortified by the Hero's immunities. She was just Ruti, a normal young woman fretting over the scene before us.

"Hmmm."

I looked closely at the tiny buds of gray starfish grass lying limply on the ground. Ruti and Tisse were growing the herb in one corner of the greenhouse. The sprouts were visibly weakened. Typically, gray starfish grass had firm roots, and the seedlings sprang up straight. Yet these ones were wilted.

"Why?" Ruti asked.

"Mold," I answered, using a trowel to scoop up some of the soil to show her. Careful examination revealed that the dirt a few centimeters below the surface had started to turn a yellow shade. "The soil's color has changed."

Ruti and Tisse stared at the soil there on the trowel.

"It's cold mold. It absorbs heat from its surroundings to grow," I explained.

"I've seen it in caves and ruins, but it was bigger then," Ruti commented.

"It's only an issue out adventuring when it's thriving in large colonies."

Cold mold was one of the many types of fungi that grew throughout the continent. It was a unique specimen that absorbed the warmth of its surroundings to reproduce. When its radius extended past half a meter, it was called a *colony*, and when the radius reached ten meters, it was referred to as a *territory*. At that size, any source of heat—including living creatures—that drew near experienced sudden heat loss. It was enough that, for people who had a low blessing level, thirty seconds of exposure could make them faint.

So long as you moved away quickly to get warm, you'd be fine. However, if you were injured and unable to escape, it could be lethal.

Examining the soil, I said, "It will hardly ever grow into a colony in civilized places, but it can reproduce in small quantities in warm soil like this."

The cold mold was lowering the temperature of the dirt, causing the gray starfish grass to weaken.

"How did cold mold...," Ruti muttered.

"It was probably dormant in the soil. Normally, it hibernates during winter, and only a small amount remains. The greenhouse must have revitalized it," I surmised.

I guess you could say Ruti and Tisse had been unlucky. But it was almost a given that something unforeseen would happen during the process of changing the land over to a new crop. Undoubtedly, a few more problems would also arise during the first year.

"..." Ruti slumped over sadly.

"Since you noticed it so quickly, there might still be time to take some countermeasures," I encouraged.

"Countermeasures? The plants can be saved?"

"Yeah, though there's no guarantee."

Cold mold was dangerous, but from what I observed, it hadn't spread too much. Unlike molds that directly parasitized plants, if you removed the cold mold and then raised the temperature of the soil again, the crops had a chance at survival.

Because Ruti had recognized the issue this morning and come to me immediately, I believed there was enough time to rescue the herbs.

"We've gotta strike quickly. I'll prepare something to kill off the cold mold," I said.

"Okay!"

Leaving the farm to Tisse, Ruti and I quickly went to buy the ingredients I needed.

* * *

After diluting the necessary chemical several times over, we carefully spread it around the plot and then checked the condition below the surface. Things appeared to be going our way. Fortunately, cold mold was not especially resilient. If all went well, it would be gone by the next morning.

"After making sure the mold is dead from the soil tomorrow, you should lay out coarse fabric over the ground to warm it up some," I advised.

"Got it." Ruti clenched her fists in front of her chest as she answered. There was a powerful determination in her eyes. She wanted to save those medicinal herb sprouts.

Ironically, she'd never displayed that kind of conviction while she was the Hero.

"You did well to notice it."

"Mhm."

I started to reach my hand out to pat her head.

"Whoops."

I stopped myself, though. My hand was dirty from working with the soil. I couldn't mess up my sister's clean blue locks.

Ruti pouted when she saw me stop. "Mrgh." She grabbed my hand with both of hers, pulling it over and placing it on her head.

"You'll get dirty."

"I'll take a bath after, so it's fine."

She pressed her head against my palm, as if to confirm the feel of it. I couldn't help smiling at that.

"Fine, I get it. You did great, Ruti. That's my little sister for you," I praised her while petting her head gently, hoping not to get her too messy.

"Mhm, I'm your little sister."

The corners of Ruti's mouth curved slightly as she smiled happily.

I was hit by the urge to wrap her in a big hug when I saw her cute little gesture. However, I managed to contain myself.

*　　　*　　　*

When I departed the greenhouse, I saw Tisse sitting down to feed Mister Crawly Wawly an insect after she had finished taking care of the other herbs she and Ruti were raising.

"Thanks for your help… Is everything all right?"

"Yeah. Good thing you two caught the problem so quickly. Some of the sprouts are probably going to go bad, but the majority will recover."

"That's good." Tisse breathed a sigh of relief.

Mister Crawly Wawly spread his legs, slumping his stomach to the ground in apparent relief. I grinned at the sight.

"Mister Crawly Wawly felt guilty that he didn't notice the cold mold sooner. He said he would've recognized it immediately had he walked over the soil," Tisse explained.

He did seem to be a bit down. Almost sad.

"I see. Getting his help with managing things might be a good idea going forward," I replied.

There probably weren't many farmers who could sense the dirt's condition as well as he could.

In apparent response to what I said, Mister Crawly Wawly spun his front legs as if to declare, "I'll do my best!"

"Red." Tisse stood up, looking me straight in the eye. "Before I met all of you, I would never have imagined such a tranquil daily life working the land. The old me wouldn't have been comfortable spending time like this with an enemy ship so close by. Truthfully, I may have simply assassinated Prince Salius."

The words were in jest, but if Tisse ever got serious, that would likely be a simple feat for her. Her eyes narrowed ever so slightly; the changes in her expression were as minor as always.

"I like this, though."

"I see."

Seeing the barely recognizable smile on her face, I grinned, too.

Tisse was a precious friend.

* * *

At noon, I left the shop to Rit and went over to see Yarandrala.

"Red!" Spotting me from far away, she ran straight over instead of just waving. "You came!"

She didn't bother to slow down at all, charging straight into a big hug. I smiled awkwardly as I supported her weight.

"Tch… Red, you jerk…"

The workers nearby glared at me with scary looks in their eyes!

You've got it wrong! High elves just get overly touchy with friends! It isn't what you think!

My mental excuses floated into the Zoltan sky without reaching anyone, however.

I finally peeled Yarandrala away and managed to get a look at how the work was proceeding.

"How are the coconut trees?" I inquired.

"They're fine," Yarandrala responded, puffing out her chest. "Each is brimming with vitality. We're only harvesting the coconuts to make a couple of months' worth of oil. I know the people in Zoltan like to take it easy, but they're listening to my instructions and taking proper care of the plants. So I've got no complaints!"

"Great! Thank you, Yarandrala!"

"You're welcome. I'm glad I could help!"

When it came to caring for the trees we were using to harvest coconuts for oil, Yarandrala was more knowledgeable and skilled than the botanists in Central. She had researched how much would be best to gather from how many trees and had drawn up a plan that anyone could comprehend.

"Heh-heh," Yarandrala chuckled happily. "This is the first time you've come to ask me for assistance with plants instead of something connected to fighting or adventures."

"Only because my life was nonstop combat until I came here."

"I'm glad. Really I am. I always wanted to try growing things with you."

She wrapped her arms around my neck, gazed into my eyes, and beamed.

"When the stuff with Lilinrala is cleared up, let's raise some flowers together. I'm sure the ones we grow will bloom beautifully."

Yarandrala kissed my cheek and then returned to the workers.

"Growing flowers, huh? Seems she's taken a liking to Zoltan, too." I smiled while watching her go.

Being inundated by hateful glares was getting frightening, however, so I decided to make for the oil refinery.

Despite the name, it was only a gazebo that kept out the sun. Laborers were extracting oil from the coconuts. They were using the recipe I had designed, so I looked around and gave a few people some advice.

"It doesn't look like there are any problems here."

Everyone was working hard, even in the chilly air of winter. It was a rather un-Zoltan-like show of effort.

"If only they were so serious all the time… Nah, that would get too stressful, I guess."

"Yes, I agree," came a familiar voice. Turning around, I saw the trader I had spoken to at the Merchants Guild. Apparently, the guild had tasked him with observing the operation. "Folks are working diligently because the job's only just begun. Once they get used to it, they'll remember to slack off here and there.

Scratching my cheek, I responded, "Ha-ha, that's a bit of a problem, though I guess it fits for Zoltan."

"We've already distributed several barrels, and the response has been favorable. It doesn't have the odor of fish oil, so there were some who wanted to make the switch to coconut oil going forward."

"That's good to hear."

"Thankfully, it doesn't seem as though we'll have an issue with supplies, despite that Veronian ship's best efforts. It would be deadly for business if the market stagnated, but as long as there is still something to move, we'll get by."

"Income will drop, though," I commented.

"The guild will manage things with subsidies to keep people from going under completely," the merchant assured. The incident had likely hit him harder than anyone, yet his face remained bright. "This is all because of you and Rit. You have my gratitude."

Appreciation for Red the apothecary instead of Gideon and his sword—I couldn't explain it, but it made me very happy.

* * *

After that, I went back to the shop.

The customers were sparse, so I chatted casually while selling them whatever medicine they required.

Although worried about the Veronian battleship, the people of Zoltan retained their "it will figure itself out tomorrow" personalities and went about their daily lives.

After closing up in the evening, Rit and I had a nice dinner with Ruti, Tisse, and Yarandrala, and after the three of them left, Rit and I got into the bath together to wash.

We took our time to get warm, and I made some hot milk while Rit cared for her hair.

It was just our normal, everyday life.

After the sun had gone down, I sat under the moonlight and took care of my sword. The bronze blade was resistant to rust, unlike steel ones. Most of the time, all it really needed was a quick wiping with a cloth.

"I just bought a new one, but it's already nicked." It had gotten pretty beat up from the fights with the gem beast and the stray assassins. Recently, it seemed we'd been up against quite a few powerful opponents, and the stuff with Veronia hadn't been resolved yet. "The core still seems all right, though."

I wanted to show the sword a little more appreciation, so I pulled out some whetstones and got a bucket of water. I sharpened the blade using two whetstones with different coarsenesses.

Tisse's shortsword was sharp enough that just touching its blade was enough to cut skin, but my sword didn't have nearly as keen an edge. Honing it was really only a minor touch-up.

The process didn't take long. I rinsed the blade off when I was done, polished it with the cloth, and then held it beneath the moonlight.

"I'm sure you never imagined going up against enemies like those."

A weapon like this was meant for rookies just getting started. It was to be used against goblins and lesser slimes. After half a year, it would be traded in for a better weapon and then purchased secondhand by another novice, becoming their first partner…

Sitting there, I swung the sword down once. It cut through the air with a whistle and caught the pale light from outside.

"It's not like I've gone out looking for battles…but not fighting for my friends just because I want to live freely feels limiting. Sorry, but I'm probably going to need you again sometime."

"Very well. If thou wouldst wield us in a battle that thou dost desire, we wouldst wish no more," an echoing voice replied.

I chuckled at that. "Oh? Who might you be, one who answers my request?"

"Hah-hah-hah. I am the spirit that dwellest in this sword of bronze. I recognize thou hast cherished me. Be it for the sake of thy sister and her companion, thy friends in Zoltan, or for thy most beloved, if I am of service in protection of them, then use us as thou wouldst."

"Thank you very much, Sir Spirit."

The spirit laughed again.

"I have one final counsel for thee."

"What is it?"

The self-proclaimed spirit of the bronze sword standing behind me wrapped my head in a big hug.

"Thou shouldst be true to thy desires towards thy beloved!"

Rit squeezed me tight.

"What do you mean 'desires'…? Huh? Something feels different."

"Eh-heh-heh."

Rit felt odd, almost fluffy…

"Are you using Aspect of Wolf?"

"Bingo. Come on. I know you've wanted to pet me since the moment you saw me like this! Or, more precisely, you wanted to get all lovey-dovey!"

There were bushy wolf ears on Rit's head, and a fluffy tail was peeking out from her skirt.

How does that work with her underwear? I wondered. Shape spells temporarily subsumed the user's clothes into their body while transformed, but aspects spells were supposed to leave the clothes unchanged. It was too embarrassing to ask, of course, but I couldn't help speculating.

"Why don't you feel for yourself." Rit grinned as she slipped onto my lap.

"E-even if you say that…"

Rit wriggled her tail, enjoying my agitation. For some reason, it felt like she was being particularly aggressive today.

"You've been troubled about things a bit lately, haven't you?"

"...You noticed?"

"Nothing gets past Wolf Rit's nose."

Rit turned, her knees pressing against my stomach as she sat facing me on my lap.

"I don't have an answer for your worries about the world or Divine Blessings. All I can do is tell you that you've made the right decision." She smiled before pressing her forehead against mine. "I'm glad you're here, so this can't be wrong."

"I guess so..."

Rit and I were happy.

No matter what life we lived, staying true to that was the right answer for us.

"So pamper me more now!"

Rit kissed my cheek... Her tongue felt different.

I was a little surprised.

"Uh, ummm..."

"Come on already. You wanted to pet me like this, right?"

Rit looked down, slightly pointing the top of her head toward me as her wolf ears twitched.

"You're coming on pretty strong tonight..." Despite what I said, I was enjoying things, too. I was working hard to restrain myself, however, because my love was threatening to go wild.

I started out patting Rit's head gently, taking care not to mess up her blond locks. However, judging by her expression, that wasn't enough, so I stroked her more firmly, like playing with a dog. Rit's tail wagged in response. Her eyes narrowed, and her lips spread into a little smile.

Aspect of Wolf was magic for battle. It granted a wolf's enhanced senses and physical abilities to gain an edge in combat. The assassins from before had employed Aspect of Riding Drake to fight, too. The vast majority of magic and skills were for combat.

Yet Rit was using it to cheer me up—to acquire a wolf's cool, charming appearance and personality instead of its physical capabilities.

I doubt whatever great mage who first developed that spell in the distant past envisioned it being utilized this way. That brought me joy. It was like magic that Rit had created for me alone.

No longer satisfied with just being pet, Rit wrapped her arms around me, hugging me and rubbing her cheek against mine.

Sitting there hugging each other like that… The sense of closeness was incredible. I couldn't begin to describe the swell of emotions, but it was a wonderful sensation.

All of my worries about fighting seemed tiny by comparison. It felt like Rit's body was a bit hotter than usual in Aspect of Wolf mode. That warmth was pleasant on a cool winter's night.

"Why not feel how the tail works?" Rit suggested, twisting her tail in my lap.

"If you're going to insist, then I guess I have to."

"Eh-heh-heh. Be my guest!"

Rit clung tighter to me. Looking over her shoulder, I could see the beautiful curve of her back down to her bottom, and her tail sticking out from below her skirt. I couldn't see from my position, but with the hem raised that much, her underwear had to be showing.

Aspect of Wolf was truly glorious magic, but maybe it was too much for humans. It was only the two of us, however.

"It's okay, I have a wolf's ears and nose. I'll know if anyone comes by," Rit assured before kissing my cheek over and over.

I couldn't hold it in anymore and squeezed Rit tight. She returned the gesture just as powerfully.

It was a wonderful moment.

I reached my hand down to Rit's tail. My heart started beating faster. The only way to know how the tail worked was to reach into her skirt.

How (*swish*) did (*swish*) her (*swish, swish*) tail (*swish, swish, swish, swish, swish*)…

"Rit."

"Wh-what?"

"Your tail is wagging too hard. I can't get any closer."

It was moving so much that I feared it might break. Rit's face turned bright red.

"No fair!" she cried, and she pushed me down. "It's not fair. I made sure you couldn't see my face, but my tail betrayed me."

She was rubbing her face against my cheek and jaw. I guess her emotions were getting a bit wolf-like. The power of the magic must have been why she was acting forward today.

Rit finally stopped rubbing against my chest and face and pulled back slightly. She was on top of my chest as I lay down on the ground, her cheeks flushed. The sight of her there was too cute for me to handle.

"You know, I'll probably lock myself away in the bedroom from embarrassment tomorrow," she admitted.

"Yeah, I can see that happening," I agreed.

"So…"

"Uh huh?"

"I want to cuddle with you extra today to make up for it," Rit said, grinning.

Her altered appearance was truly too exciting.

"As long as you're with me, I couldn't be happier," I confessed, letting my feelings spill out offhandedly. That was just how riled up I was.

Rit beamed, and her tail moved slowly in a wide arc.

"I love you," Rit whispered.

I couldn't take it anymore.

Maybe I should ask her if she can use Aspect of Cat some other time…

Epilogue

Lilinrala's Resolve

Birds were chirping outside the window, signaling the dawn of the following day.

I opened my eyes, coming face-to-face with Rit sleeping beside me.

I was the only one in the world who could see this side of the woman known as Rit the hero. She was resting defenselessly with such a tranquil look on her face.

Between half-conscious thoughts like that, a feeling of joy welled up inside me, and I gently pressed my forehead to hers. The building happiness spread through my chest.

"Nfgh."

Rit broke into a little smile, like she was having a pleasant dream.

It seemed the feeling in me had spread to her, and I grinned like a fool. It was a good thing no one else was around.

I should sleep a bit longer.

After what had happened last night, I wouldn't be able to cuddle up with Rit today.

I closed my eyes, and as a result, I could sense her presence against my skin all the more acutely. I basked in the peaceful moment as I dozed off.

* * *

"Red."

A voice whispered in my ear.

The pleasant tickle caused me to stir. When I moved, my head pressed against something soft. It felt good, so I reached out with both arms, seeking that warm feeling, and then I slipped back to slumber again.

"...I guess we can sleep in a bit longer," a distant voice said.

* * *

There was a knock. It was coming from the door to the shop.

Rit and I opened our eyes at the same time.

"G-good morning."

"Good morning..."

Rit's large chest, enclosed in her pajamas, was right in front of my eyes.

At some point, I had fallen asleep with my face in her soft, warm bosom.

Rit was holding my head, caressing near the nape of my neck.

We looked at each other, cheeks red.

"T-that's probably Ruti and the others!" she said, frazzled.

"Y-yeah, we really overslept, I guess! I'll start getting breakfast ready!" I hastily replied.

I hurried out of the bedroom. I needed to let our guests in.

"Coming!" I called out as I headed to the entrance. "All right, time for another day's work."

I could tell I was still grinning idiotically.

* * *

"Okay, what can I make on short order?"

I crossed my arms in thought while I stood in the kitchen. The oven wasn't even hot yet, meaning toasting bread would take a while. There wasn't time to prepare soup, either.

"Hmm. In that case..."

I lit the stove and got bread, onions, tomato, cheese, ham, and some butter.

After cutting the bread, I added sliced onions and tomatoes, and then put the cheese and ham on top. Black pepper sufficed for seasoning.

Once that was done, I melted some butter in a frying pan. I put the sandwich onto the pan and weighted it with a small pot. The smell of bread toasting made my sleepy body feel hungry. Fortunately, I wouldn't have to wait too long.

"That should be about right."

The bread was a nice toasty brown. I cut it diagonally, and with that, the hot sandwich was complete. The melted cheese oozed out slightly from the cut.

"Okay, now to take care of the rest."

I went about my task swiftly in order to satisfy everyone's empty stomachs.

"""""Thanks for the food!"""""

Ruti, Tisse, Rit, and I were all gathered around the table.

Mister Crawly Wawly put his front legs together and bowed his head in front of the mosquito he'd caught, too. What a polite spider.

"Mgh."

The cheese stretched from Rit's sandwich as she took a bite. She wound the long strand up and then took another bite. Evidently, she was enjoying it.

Tisse was cutting her sandwich neatly with a knife and fork. Her expression betrayed nothing, but judging by how quickly she was eating, she liked the food, too.

Ruti was looking back and forth between the two of them, head cocked in confusion.

"Ruti?" I asked.

"Umm, Big Brother, how are you supposed to eat this?"

"However you want to is fine."

"Okay." Ruti stared at her sandwich for a few seconds. "Mph." She chose to eat the same way as Rit. The moment it reached her mouth, her expression brightened like a switch had been flipped.

* * *

After Ruti, Tisse, and Mister Crawly Wawly left for their farm, Rit and I started preparing for the workday.

"..."

Rit's face had been red for a while, and she hadn't said anything.

She was likely thinking about last night. Glancing over at me, she writhed as she covered her mouth with her bandana.

So cute.

"Oh yeah, we have to deliver medicine to Dr. Newman today! I'll get things. Can I leave the storefront to you, Rit?"

"Y-yeah, sure. If anything, it would be easier to get over this if I had a little time to myself."

"Hah, okay, got it. But first..." I ran over to Rit and kissed her cheek.

"Hyah?!"

Rit would normally have been able to handle that much, but today she was blushing madly.

She was so cute.

"All right, the shop's in your hands!"

"You're so mean."

I headed to the storage room while watching Rit dive behind the counter to hide.

With Dr. Newman's note in one hand, I went through our stock to prepare his order.

"That's all of our stock of coca leaves. Are there any left in the yard?" I muttered.

I could worry about that once I got back. Our sales had risen lately, so ingredients were running low more quickly.

"And the last thing is medicine to help with fevers. All right, that's everything."

I checked one last time to make sure I had everything.

"Okay, Rit! I'm done here! Need help with anything?"

"Check the change, please."

"Got it."

Her cheeks were still scarlet, but she handled her job just fine.

We had gotten used to opening together. Fortunately, our frantic rush ended soon, and we were ready for business at the usual time.

"Let's have—"

"—another good day. Eh-heh-heh."

We laughed together as we pumped our fists.

Just like always.

*　　*　　*

In a room on the Veronian warship.

The high elf Lilinrala, once feared by countless nations as the leader of the Elven Corsairs, was scowling. The frown didn't mar her beauty, however, even though she had long since passed the point of being considered a young woman by high elf standards.

"My subordinates were caught, and there's been no contact from the assassin."

Stoic though she was, Lilinrala could not help but worry.

She had deployed some of the strongest people in Veronia, well-suited for solo fights or group combat. They were capable enough that they even stood a chance against an A-rank adventurer.

The assassins she'd hired were supposed to be top-notch, too. Archmage or not, Misphia shouldn't have escaped unscathed.

I'm worried about the safety of my subordinates, but more importantly, just who the hell are Tifa and Ruhr?

Lilinrala had gathered information around Zoltan about the two adventurers over the past few days, but it was entirely unreliable.

What is this place?

When it was necessary to investigate someone quickly, the best method was to inquire with someone who had done the same earlier. Normally, if a person who stood out as much as Ruhr or Tifa showed up, someone would take the time to look into their history. And yet, Lilinrala's minions couldn't find anyone who had investigated Tifa. Even the Thieves Guild had been a dead end.

It's possible the locals are wary enough to play dumb…

However, Lilinrala couldn't imagine that this little city in the middle of nowhere was home to folks proficient enough to deceive spies she had gathered to protect King Geizeric.

Ruhr and Tifa are outsiders far stronger than everyone else in Zoltan. Doesn't that bother these people?

In the end, all Lilinrala uncovered was that the two young women were extremely capable adventurers. Any specifics about their pasts were shrouded in mystery. The high elf was at her wit's end.

"Which means this guy is the key, then."

He was probably the only person in Zoltan who could help her.

Had Lilinrala known about him before her subordinates got caught, she would have targeted him over the self-proclaimed white knight Ruhr.

"Red, the apothecary."

Lilinrala stood, opening a locked box and taking out a pair of dimly radiant green high-elf steel gauntlets.

"Blood of the proud high elves that flows through my veins, lend me strength."

The gauntlets were a magic item passed down through Lilinrala's family. By equipping them, the wearer gained all of the sword skills of their ancestors.

Even a novice became a master with the wondrous objects, but Lilinrala was a first-rate swordsman in her own right and had a high blessing level as well. When she wore the gauntlets, she surpassed the realm of experts and stood on par with legends.

She also retrieved a longsword different from her usual cutlass. Its sheath was white, adorned with vibrant gold decorations. When Lilinrala drew the blade slightly, the wind magic confined within surged out, rustling her silver hair.

The ensorcelled weapon was yet another family heirloom. It was said that a famed elven smith had forged it using his very life to fuel the flames. Its name was Elven Sorrow, owing to the blacksmith's lament at the many lives the sword would claim.

"I'll have to go myself."

Despite being Ruhr's older brother and a friend of Tifa's, Red was only a D-rank adventurer. Yet reports indicated he was likely hiding his true strength. There was no mistaking that he was at least on par with a C-ranker.

Naturally, Lilinrala still had many underlings capable of easily capturing a C-rank adventurer. However, given the recent failures, Lilinrala elected to handle the matter herself.

They don't seem ready to hand over the holy church registers yet, but I have to finish off Misphia before they change their minds.

Lilinrala readied her magic items as a dark resolve filled her heart.

Afterword

To everyone who has picked up this book, thank you very much! I'm Zappon, the author.

Thanks to all of your support, this series has reached its sixth volume!

I'm so excited to continue sharing this tale with everyone. Hopefully, it lives up to your expectations.

This book was a bit of a struggle. I fretted over the plot and the writing, and I rewrote parts of it multiple times.

Unfortunately, there's no guarantee that a story will become better the harder you work on it, but there is a certain profoundly moving feeling that comes with completing something after a struggle, so I have a bit of an emotional attachment to this book. I hope it will be an enjoyable read for you.

The sixth volume is all about problems that, under normal circumstances, the Hero would've resolved.

With the Hero's aid, the allied forces would gradually gain the upper hand. At which point, the next problem would be the Kingdom of Veronia, which had betrayed humanity and sided with the demon lord's army. In order to stop a war between humans, the Hero would infiltrate Veronia to talk sense into the leadership there.

The old king would be on his sickbed, and an evil queen would be taking advantage to act as she pleased. The key to resolving the issue would lie with the previous queen, who disappeared fifty years ago.

That story would see the Hero flying on her airship and traveling around the continent in search of the lost queen. In that version of things, Zoltan would just be a town where a villager casually mentions, "An old woman lives out in the forest to the west of town."

Obviously, Red and Ruti's tale did not end up like that.

Should Ruti have continued the Hero's journey? What are the costs of the Hero electing to live freely? How will people react to Red and Ruti's decision? That's what this story is about.

Tragedy doesn't fit a slow life setting, so I hope you can relax and enjoy the tales of Red and his friends' day-to-day life.

The most important highlight was when Rit used her transformation for something other than practical combat enhancements, and we got to see Wolf Rit and Red share a lovey-dovey scene!

By the way, the third volume of Ikeno Masahiro's manga version of *Banished from the Hero's Party,* serialized in Monthly Shonen Ace, is also on sale.

It's releasing at almost the same time as this volume, and it covers the end of the first light novel. The scene from the climax, where Ruti snaps and punches Ares, was even more impressive than I had imagined! She really let him have it!

Please check out the manga as well!

We've got the seventh volume coming next.

After her minions and the assassins failed, the high elf pirate Lilinrala sets foot in Zoltan herself. From Prince Salius to Queen Leonor, little Zoltan has certainly gotten wrapped up in some high-profile political intrigue. Plus, there's that connection between Red and Queen Leonor, too. Expect a story of Red and his friends' slow life during the end of winter and the arrival of spring!

I hope you will continue to support this series when the next volume arrives.

* * *

This book could not have been completed without the help of many people.

One of the reasons I wanted to write about a wolf-eared version of Rit is that I wanted to see Yasumo's illustrations. Thank you for such wonderful pictures!

To the designers, proofreaders, printers, and everyone involved in the actual production, this book exists thanks to all of you. Thank you very much.

To this series' editor, Miyakawa, can you believe we've reached the sixth installment?

Seeing the number of light novels published every month, I've learned just how incredible it is to have readers pick up my works from among all the others. It's our combined effort that has made that possible. I hope we can continue that as we push forward!

And finally, it's the readers who give the most value to a book. If you got even a little bit of pleasure out of reading this light novel, then I am satisfied as an author.

Zappon

Swooning from the hectic end of the year, 2019

This is Yasumo, the illustrator.
Wolf Rit was refreshing and fun to draw!

The decisive confrontation with the looming Veronian threat draws near! Will Red manage to preserve his peaceful days?

ON SALE: FALL 2022!

HAVE YOU BEEN TURNED ON TO LIGHT NOVELS YET?

IN STORES NOW!

SWORD ART ONLINE, VOL. 1–24
SWORD ART ONLINE PROGRESSIVE 1–8

The chart-topping light novel series that spawned the explosively popular anime and manga adaptations!

MANGA ADAPTATION AVAILABLE NOW!

ACCEL WORLD, VOL. 1–25

Prepare to accelerate with an action-packed cyber-thriller from the bestselling author of *Sword Art Online*.

MANGA ADAPTATION AVAILABLE NOW!

SPICE AND WOLF, VOL. 1–22

A disgruntled goddess joins a traveling merchant in this light novel series that inspired the *New York Times* bestselling manga.

MANGA ADAPTATION AVAILABLE NOW!